THE DARING ONE

A Billionaire Bride Pact Romance

CAMI CHECKETTS

Birch River Publishing

The Daring One: A Billionaire Bride Pact Romance

COPYRIGHT ©2017 by Camille Coats Checketts

Birch River Publishing

Smithfield, Utah

Published in the United States of America

Cover design: Christina Dymock

Interior design: Memphis Checketts

Editing: Daniel Coleman

To my running buddies—Jennalyn and Missy. Thank you for making me laugh, forcing me run much faster than I want to, and brainstorming fun ideas for my writing.

INTRODUCTION BY LUCY MCCONNELL

I've heard it said that some people come into your life and quickly leave—others leave footprints on your heart. Jeanette and Cami are two wonderful authors and women who have left their mark on my heart. Their overwhelming support, knowledge, and general goodness have pushed me forward as a writer and nurtured me as a friend. That's why I'm pleased to introduce you to their new and innovative series: The Billionaire Bride Pact Romances.

In each story, you'll find romance and character growth. I almost wrote personal growth—forgetting these are works of fiction—because the books we read become a part of us, their words stamped into our souls. As with any good book, I disappeared into the pages for a while and was able to walk sandy beaches, visit a glass blowing shop, and spend time with a group of women who had made a pact—a pact that influenced their lives, their loves, and their dreams.

I encourage you to put your feet up, grab a cup of something wonderful, and fall in love with a billionaire today.

Wishing you all the best,
Lucy McConnell

THE BILLIONAIRE BRIDE PACT

I, Summer Anderson, do solemnly swear that I will marry a billionaire and live happily ever after. If I fail to meet my pledge, I will stand up at my wedding reception and sing the Camp Wallakee theme song.

CHAPTER ONE

SUMMER PLODDED ALONG THE SNODGRASS TRAIL, WAITING FOR THE promised views of Mt. Crested Butte, but so far it was a dirt path with lots of lush greenery—mostly aspen and pine trees. Crested Butte, Colorado, was beautiful, and she didn't completely loathe exploring the trails on foot, but she would've traded Diet Coke for life to be on a mountain bike. Sadly, she couldn't afford a mountain bike or an abundance of Diet Coke. Maybe after she got her first paycheck from Haley she could rent a bike for a day and go on a huge excursion with only Diet Coke in her water bottle. She laughed at herself, thinking of the bellyache she'd have.

At least when she was running, she was in tune with Mother Earth and all that schmuck. Her younger self would've been happily running barefoot, but she'd become disillusioned with branches and rocks poking her soles, and honestly, Mother Nature hadn't been too kind to her lately. With her earbuds in, jamming to Mumford & Sons, she was only in sync with nature visually, but she couldn't pound through miles on foot without some tunes.

She sensed movement behind her and jumped in surprise as she heard someone yell, "On your left!"

She dodged to the right, but the biker's front tire clipped her heel and she went sprawling into the undergrowth. Branches and rocks scratched at her face and bare arms. Summer let loose a yelp and rolled onto her back with a groan.

She stared up through aspen leaves to the blue sky above, yanking her earbuds out. "Ouch," she muttered, inhaling the scent of dirt and pine needles, not ready to move quite yet.

Footsteps pounded toward her, and then a man wearing a bicycle helmet and sunglasses bent over her. "You all right?" he panted out, pulling off his sunglasses and helmet and staring intently at her.

Summer blinked up at him. She must've hit her head really hard. Was it even possible that Channing Tatum had come to her rescue? She shook her head and blinked quickly. It couldn't be the actor she'd daydreamed about from *Dear John* and *The Vow*. She'd even watched G.I. Joe movies to drool over him some more. This guy looked exactly like him, with the perfectly proportioned, manly face. There was a slight dimple in his cheek, even though he wasn't smiling. His beautiful teal-colored eyes looked much too concerned. Wait. Weren't Channing Tatum's eyes more of a true green?

"Are you all right?" he asked again.

"Not dead yet," she muttered.

He chuckled, and that irresistible dimple got deeper. "Your back and neck aren't hurt?"

She nodded, then shook her head, a bit awestruck. Was it really him? Crested Butte was a cool spot; maybe celebrities vacationed here. But wasn't Channing Tatum married? Dang. She'd better stop ogling him.

Reaching a hand underneath her upper back, he gently lifted her to a seated position. Warmth spread where his hand lingered on her back. From the way her body reacted to that simple touch, she certainly hoped he wasn't a married and/or a famous actor. She wondered if he was gagging at the sweat that had seeped through her shirt. Tempted to sniff her armpits, she could only hope Secret antiperspirant was doing a bang-up job and she didn't reek too bad.

"Can you stand?" he asked in a deep rumble. He sounded like Channing Tatum too. Oh, wow. Maybe fate had stopped hating on her.

"I'll give it my A game," she said.

He laughed, kept one hand on her back, and took her other hand, helping her to her feet. He released her hand, but kept his palm on her back. For support, or was he feeling zing too? "You made it," he said.

She stared into those greenish-blue eyes and sighed. "Yes, I did." They stood there looking at each other for a few blissful seconds. She couldn't resist asking, "Are you Channing Tatum?"

His deep laughter cascaded over her. He shook his head and said, "No."

"Oh. You probably get that a lot?"

"A bit." He grinned, and that dimple deepened.

Summer felt relief wash over her. Yay that he wasn't Channing Tatum, because even though that would've been rocking cool to meet him, if he wasn't the famous actor, that meant this guy was available. Oh, yeah. "So you aren't married, right?" she demanded. Then her eyes widened. *Oh my. Stop, mouth!*

His chuckle was a little more awkward this time, and he pulled his hand back. "No."

"Oh, good. I thought you were Channing Tatum and he's married, so I was feeling all awkward that I was checking you out and ..." Her face flared red as she finally clamped her traitorous mouth shut.

He smiled again and arched an eyebrow. "You were checking me out?"

"Whew. I think it's time for my mouth to stop running and my legs to remember the action."

"Wait." He placed a warm hand on her arm. "Are you sure you're okay?"

Summer had to think about it. She patted her lopsided ponytail, ran her hand over her scratched face, and cringed as she noticed some small cuts on her arms. "I think the permanent damage is a minimum. Why'd you run me off the trail?"

"Uh," he kind of grunted out in what sounded like surprise. "I'm sorry. I came around the corner and there you were. I yelled twice and tried to swerve around you." He glanced at the earbuds dangling from her neck. "Maybe your music was too loud?"

She bristled. "Maybe you should slow down or try using your own two legs for a change."

"Whoa ... What?"

She tilted her head to the side and her long hair brushed her arm. "You know what they say: Those who can't run, bike."

He gave another surprised half-grunt, half-laugh.

Summer flipped her hair, gave him a sassy look, and took off running down the trail. She didn't look back to see if he was coming. Her left knee was aching. Did she slam it into the ground, or had his bike tire hit higher than she remembered? It was all a blur, and it really didn't matter. She had to keep running and save some face. She didn't want that incredibly handsome man to know that she'd give anything to be the one on the bike. Her opportunity to make good money and have incredible adventures with her best friend, Taylor, were gone, but she still had her pride.

Seconds later, she heard his bike approaching. Shoot. She increased her pace, but it was dumb to imagine a runner could outpace a bike. If she was going uphill then she might stand a chance, but this part of the trail was pretty level.

The biker stayed right behind her as she flew over the trail, ignoring him. Within a few minutes she was panting for air. She made a split decision and dodged off to the side of the trail, gestured for him to go past, and yelled, "Bike on through, oh high and mighty one!"

The man slammed on his brakes and pulled level with her. His helmet and sunglasses were back on so she couldn't read his expression, but that attractive—scratch that, infuriating—smirk and dimple were in place. "High and mighty one?"

"All you bikers think you're superior or something," she huffed out. "I'll have you know I've done both, and running is a million times more miserable. I mean, challenging."

He took off the sunglasses, and she was happy to see those teal-colored eyes again. No, she was happy she could tell what he was thinking more easily. "I'd agree with miserable. Why don't you bike, then?"

"None of your beeswax, dude. Move along." She shooed him with her hands.

His smirk turned into an all-out grin. "I'm sorry, but I need to make sure you get home safe, seeing how I caused your injury and all."

Summer planted her hands on her hips. She'd protected herself from handsome men in more countries than this yahoo knew decorated the world map. "Listen, buddy. I've got Mace and I am very proficient at using it."

His eyebrows shot up again and he raised his hands. "Whoa. I'm not, no, I wouldn't try to ... do anything."

"And *I'm* going to take the strange man's word for that? I forgave you for knocking me down, but you try and follow me home, and you'll see this tough woman kick your well-formed butt. Comprende?"

He laughed at her again, but quickly wiped the mirth off his face when she whipped her pepper spray out of her pocket. "Hey. Okay. I just wanted to make sure you're all right. My mother taught me to be a gentleman."

"Big claim, preppy boy."

"Being a gentleman?"

"For sure. Every guy claims they're a gentleman until they get a chance to take advantage when a woman's alone and they think she's defenseless."

"Sheesh." He clung to his handlebars. "Defensive much?"

"You have no idea." She raised the spray. "Now are you moving, or am I leaving you in a cloud of this?"

He shook his head and stood his ground. Hmm. He was a brave one, she'd give him that. "You go," he said. "I'll follow at a safe distance to make sure you get safely out of the woods. I promise I won't follow you home."

Summer took a deep breath and nodded. She was being a tad bit overcautious. He hadn't really given off any vibes that he would hurt her, but she'd wised up over the last couple of years. She used to trust and have fun kissing any handsome man that came along, but she'd learned a woman needed to be wary and always have ways to protect herself. Luckily, she'd been able to protect herself, find help, or escape when the need arose.

"Thanks," she muttered. She pocketed her pepper spray and took off running again, keeping a decent pace, and trying to ignore the fact that he was behind her. Several uncomfortable miles later, she exited the trees and could see the town of Crested Butte and the beautiful valley spread out below her. She'd completely missed any amazing views she was supposed to see on the run. Dang that man's good-looking face.

She went off the side of the trail and gestured him through again. The man stopped. What? Did he want her to thank him or something?

"Sorry about running you off the trail," he said.

"It's under the bridge," she muttered.

He took off his sunglasses and his eyes swept over her face. She self-consciously touched one of the scratches that was stinging from her sweat. "You sure you're okay?"

"I'm tougher than a few twigs," she said.

"I can see that." He smiled. "Could I ... see you again sometime?"

Summer's eyes widened. He was definitely hitting on her now. With his looks—and his money train, from the fact that his bike and gear were top-of-the-line—he could probably snag any woman he blessed with a second glance of those ocean-colored eyes. Unfortunately for him, she'd been through her share of handsome men and she was on a siesta. Her friends from Camp Wallakee would never believe it, but it was time. She needed to figure out how to be successful as Summer, not as some dude's arm candy. Especially now that her own money train had been derailed.

"Um, no." She smiled at him. "But thanks for asking. Try again later." She tossed him another sassy look and ran off down the trail.

He pedaled up behind her. "How much later?" he asked to her back.

"You're a tourist, I assume?" She loved pretending she was a local, having lived here all of two weeks.

"Maybe."

"In town for a week?"

"Maybe."

"Try again in two weeks, then." She laughed to herself and took off running. If he wanted to stay behind her, that was his problem, not hers.

"I will," he called to her back.

Summer shook her head and kept her pace up, even though she wanted to walk more than anything in the world. The trail went for another mile, and when it ended she turned onto the road that ran down past Mt. Crested Butte and into town. The guy kept a safe distance behind her on the trail, but when she hit the road he was gone. She glanced back and saw him stopped next to a Land Rover with another Yeti mountain bike already mounted on the back rack. Yep, the guy definitely had money. He turned her way and lifted a hand. She swung her eyes forward and raced down the road. It was tragic that she'd never see him again, but probably for the best. The new Summer wasn't going to rely on anybody, especially not on a fine-looking rich dude. If only she knew how she was going to accomplish it.

CHAPTER TWO

CHANCE WATCHED THE GIRL RUNNING OFF DOWN THE STREET AND smiled to himself. She was model gorgeous with her honey-blonde hair, tan skin, deep blue eyes, and fit body, but it was her funny quips and attitude that attracted him more than her looks. Had she really pulled a canister of Mace on him? And her response when he'd asked if she was okay: "Not dead yet."

He smiled. Everyone needed humor in their lives, but he craved it. Especially after his business's latest deal. He felt like the joy had been sucked from his soul when he and his brother had helped a family company, Magical Dream Toys, become solvent, then sold it to the highest bidder. Increasing companies' value and then taking a portion of the profit upon sell was how he and his brother, Byron, had become billionaires before their thirtieth birthdays with their company Mumford's Sons. Byron had thought it was very clever naming it after Chance's favorite band and their dad.

This latest deal hadn't sat right with Chance. The company they'd sold to had promised to keep the family members on staff, but Chance had received word that they'd let them all go. Too much money in payroll was tough to keep up with, but he suspected it was the new owner's plan all along to ditch the family. The real unfortunate thing was the daughter, the toy designer, had all her designs legally locked up with the new company. She'd probably had to start all over.

Chance had called the father and creator of Magical Dream Toys, Mr. Anderson, after he heard what went down, and the older gentleman was a class act. He told Chance it was past time for him to retire anyway, and Byron had already helped Mr. Anderson's son find another position as CEO of a company that made accessory products for Apple out of Utah. The man was worried about his daughter, a "free spirit" who had been the toy designer, but he said he was certain she had a good savings account built up and she'd land on her feet; plus, it was good for her to learn how to be on her own.

Chance still felt guilty for how it had all gone down. Byron kept telling him not to worry. It was out of their hands and it was the way business went sometimes, but it still bugged Chance. He didn't have any information besides the daughter's name, Gabriella Anderson, but he'd been tempted more than once to contact her and see if he could help her find a new position. He kept putting it off because he didn't know quite what to say—*I made millions of dollars when you lost your job, can I help you?*

He secured his bike on the back of his Land Rover and drove down the hill to his rental home, which was southeast of the small downtown of Crested Butte. As he passed the girl, who was running on his route, he was tempted to honk at her like a teenager, but refrained. He waved, but she either didn't recognize him or was ignoring him. He laughed, half wanting to follow her home so he could see her again, but he'd promised not to.

Driving through Crested Butte, he thought how much he loved this town and how much his brother would hate it. The town was quiet, picturesque, and unique. Byron preferred loud, busy cities, with lots of glass and metal buildings and especially loads of beautiful, interested women.

His phone rang as he pulled into the garage. He sighed as he answered it. "Byron."

"Hey, bro. How's the first day of ... what do you call this, vacation? Or was it a monastery?"

Chance chuckled. At twenty-eight, he mostly dealt with the older brother's teasing without flaring up or calling names anymore. "They don't let beautiful women into monasteries last time I checked."

"Ooh. You gave up the vow of celibacy and found you a few hot ones?"

"One. That's all you need, one, bro." Chance had dated a lot of nice girls, but not even in the ballpark of the number of women his brother burned through, and Byron never failed to tease him about it.

He walked through the garage and into the open great room. The two-story windows gave an amazing view of the mountains on the back side of the Crested Butte Ski Resort. He might just live here year-round, bike all summer and ski all winter, and only have to deal with Byron and his latest girlfriend on the phone. It would be perfect.

"Says you. I tried one once and it didn't work. The more the merrier, right?" Byron laughed, but it sounded forced. Chance didn't know his brother had ever tried to focus on one woman for more than a couple of days. "Hey, I'm sending you some papers. I need you to check over the legalese mumbo-jumbo for me."

Chance had taken the bar exam while Byron had mastered picking up women at bars. His brother was brilliant, though, driven to the point of being a workaholic, and people loved him, especially women. Byron could also market better than anyone Chance knew, and for the most part made a great partner.

"Another company?" Chance set his water bottles in the sink and headed for the master suite, ready for a shower.

"It's a great one. The guy has created a new laptop that's lighter and honestly has better features than the Mac Air, but he's producing them for under a hundred dollars."

"That's not possible."

"He's doing it, I tell you, bro, and he just has no clue how to market the thing. You'll see from the docs, we're in negotiations for fifty-one percent of his company. He trusts us to bring in the money and the offers."

"So he wants to sell?"

"Yes, he definitely wants to sell. He can create another product and do it again, and if we play it right, he'll keep using us."

"Sounds like a dream client."

"For sure. Send those back to me by tonight?"

"You got it." Chance slipped out of his sweaty biking clothes, glad to be done with the diaper-like bike pants. It was the one downside of biking, but luckily he'd found some that didn't look quite so awful.

"How long you going to hide out in Crested Butt?"

"Butte," Chance automatically corrected, though he didn't know why. Byron would keep up the lame nickname to tease his brother. "A few weeks, maybe a month. I need to recharge."

"Whatever. As long as you keep covering *my* butt legally, I'll hold down the office for us. By the way, you don't care if I take Serena out, do you?"

Chance turned on the shower. "Byron, really? How many new secretaries are we going to have to train? Yvonne is going to kill you if you date Serena and dump her and she ends up quitting." Yvonne was their office manager and had only lasted the six years with them because she was old enough to be Byron's mother, though that didn't stop him from turning on the charm—it was just inborn with him. They paid Yvonne a lot of money to keep the business running, and to retrain secretaries after Byron broke their hearts.

"I have a good feeling about this one," his brother insisted. "You don't want to come between me and my soul mate, do you?"

Chance would've laughed if he hadn't heard the line twenty times. For some reason, the deep blue eyes of his running beauty flashed into his mind. That girl was soul mate material—witty and, from what he could tell, had some substance. Serena could barely handle transferring phone calls and occasionally transcribing a message correctly. After thirty seconds of talking to her, Chance's eyes glazed over with boredom. Byron didn't care about a soul mate. He just wanted something new and beautiful.

"I often think if Mom and Dad would've told you no more, I wouldn't have such a hard life," Chance said.

Byron laughed. "Nobody can tell me no, least of all you."

Chance sighed. It was sadly very true. He hung up before he could be accused of saying yes. Poor Serena.

CHAPTER THREE

SUMMER COULD NOT GET CHANNING TATUM'S LOOKALIKE OUT OF her mind the next two days. One problem was that manning the home décor store, Sugar 'n' Spice, for her friend, Haley, was just plain boring. It was fine when customers came in, but restocking inventory and sweeping and dusting didn't challenge Summer's brain much. She'd taken to sketching toy designs by hand or on her laptop. Haley told her that was fine as long as the customers were taken care of and the store looked good. Her friend was really kind to her, letting her stay in her little house on the farm and giving her this chance to figure out where she wanted to go from here.

Summer wasn't completely out of money, but it could easily be argued—and had been by her brother, who she'd made swear not to tell her parents she was low on funds—that she should've saved more when she'd been making great money for Magical Dream Toys as their toy designer. Especially when her Mini-Me dolls had been a top toy last Christmas and she'd raked in the royalties.

When her dad was snow-jobbed into selling and then the new owners dropped all of them within weeks, she was floored, devastated, left without any idea of where to go. She'd spent her days before the disaster designing toys, sending them on to the production team, and traveling with Taylor, who had an amazing traveling blog and actually got paid to vacation. But vacationing to exotic spots was not cheap, and Summer hadn't really been concerned with saving money.

Life had screeched to a halt with no positive cash flow and nobody willing to produce her creations. Her brother, although shocked that she hadn't stashed away more, had tried to give her money. Of course she'd blatantly refused. He needed to take care of his own family. She'd lied to her parents and told them she had plenty of money and that she was going to visit her friends in Crested Butte and figure out what direction she wanted to go next.

She was a single, smart, driven woman; she'd be fine. If she could just find another company to design for.

Haley had offered for her to come stay for the summer and work at the store. With two of her longtime friends living in the valley, Summer thought it was perfect. MacKenzie, a grade-school teacher, was married to Haley's brother, Isaac. Isaac had an innovative business with welding art, but he wasn't close to a billionaire, so MacKenzie had definitely broken the Billionaire Bride Pact the twelve friends had made at summer camp one night. Dumb teenagers, anyway. Even though MacKenzie had to sing the annoying Camp Wallakee song at her wedding as punishment, she didn't care because she was so happy. She and Isaac were much too cute.

Haley had married an extremely wealthy, extremely handsome guy named Cal, and seeing little Taz with his new dad was the best. Haley, Cal, and Taz were off traveling most of the summer, since Taz would start first grade in the fall and they'd have to actually be grounded to one location for at least five days a week. Summer loved that Haley had the opportunity to check out the world with her new husband; before she'd married Cal, she could barely afford to take her son to the beach once a year. Yet Summer had found herself spending a lot of time alone, messing up her plans of reconnecting with old friends. She usually only saw Haley and Isaac's smart-aleck dad, Trevor.

She was lonely, but at least she had her designs. She didn't know what she was going to do with all of her new ideas if she couldn't find an employer. The big companies were too hard to break into and only wanted cookie-cutter stuff anyway. She was researching some successful independents like Magical Dream Toys had been back in the happy days. There were a few options, but she wanted her portfolio bursting with new ideas before she approached one. The ornery old guy, Mr. Lillywhite, who had bought out Magical Dream Toys and fired her family, owned the rights to all her old designs. She gritted her teeth and focused on her computer.

The door dinged open and she stood to greet the customer. "Hello, welcome to Sugar 'n' ..." Her voice fell away as her jaw dropped open. "Channing Tatum," she whispered.

The guy grinned. Ooh, she loved that dimple. "It's actually Chance Judd." He covered the space between them in four long strides and stuck out his hand. His very manly, tanned hand, with just the right amount of veins to show he knew how to swing some weights around, or a hammer ... hmm, she liked the vision of the hammer. She might be drawing that tonight.

Summer put her hand in his. Yep, his hands felt as nice as they looked—warm, big, and just a hint of calluses, so you knew it truly was a manly hand and not just a wannabe. "Summer Anderson."

"Summer." He said her name so sweetly she wanted to sigh. Holding on to her hand, he turned her arm slightly. "I'm sorry about the scratches." He looked over her face too, but those had healed more quickly than her arms, and a slight covering of makeup helped too.

"It's okay. I'm a tough chick." She pulled her hand back. "What can I help you find today, sir?"

"You work here?" His greenish-blue eyes focused on her face.

Summer bristled. It wasn't such a lame job. Okay, it was, but she had higher aspirations. "Yes, sir. May I be of assistance?" She put enough bite into her voice he should've dodged out of her way.

But he was brave, or maybe just stupid, and took a step forward. "I'm sorry, it's only ... Never mind."

"Never mind what?" Summer arched an eyebrow and dared him to say it. "Spit it out, you got it that far."

"You don't seem the type to ..."

"Work as a lowly front desk girl at a home décor store?" she supplied for him. This guy was begging to get his rear kicked. "What, you thought I would be a waitress or maybe a maid at one of the resorts?" She placed both hands under her chin and curtsied submissively. He was a rich jerk, anyway.

"No. You have a very creative aura about you." He gestured to her silky tank top and flowing knee-length skirt. "Backed up by the way you dress."

"What the snot does that mean? 'Creative aura'? You're a suit. What would you know about creativity?" She did not like people who judged based on outside appearance, regardless of how fantastic his outside appearance was.

"I'm a suit?" He looked amused at her assumption. "Why do you think that?"

She gestured to his pressed khakis and button-down short-sleeved shirt. "Nobody dresses up in Crested Butte. Most people go to dinner in their hiking or biking gear. Only a suit wears crap like that on vacation."

He laughed. "You want to grab some lunch?"

Part of her wanted to say yes, but he wasn't her type—wealthy, good-looking, smart, and active didn't do it for her anymore. She smiled to herself, not believing the lie. "No, thank you. I'm working here, and even if I wasn't, I don't go to lunch with judgmental suits who think they know something about someone just because of their 'appearance.'"

He backed up a step. "Excuse me for making an assumption."

"Hmm. Nope. No excuses." She actually grinned at his shocked expression. "You sound like a lawyer."

"And that's a bad thing?" His eyebrows dipped down.

"It's a very bad thing. The last lawyers I associated with explained how I had no recourse because I had had the gall to trust someone's word. Very scary thing in the world today, trusting someone."

His face tightened, and she could see a muscle working in his jaw. "I'm sorry to hear that. Most lawyers would try to help you in a situation like that."

"You'd like to think so." She raised her nose at him. "Is there something I can help you find in the store, sir?"

Chance glanced around, then grabbed a scarf off a nearby rack and set it on the desk. "I'll take this scarf, please."

She gently rolled up the rayon-silk blue scarf. He'd picked one of her favorites. "For your girlfriend?" He'd told her he wasn't married, but there could still be a gorgeous girlfriend lingering out there. She honestly didn't care. Nope, didn't care. Okay, maybe cared a little bit.

He tilted his head to the side and studied her. "Does it matter to you who it's for?"

Summer's breath caught at the interest in his eyes. "No. I just would ... wrap it differently if it was for, say, your mom or your secretary." She bit at the side of her lip, hoping he would believe her lie as she pulled out a pink gift sack.

He softly chuckled. "I see. It's for my office manager. My brother is causing grief with our new secretary, so I'm trying to butter up Yvonne so she doesn't quit."

Summer didn't appreciate that he'd dodged the question of the girlfriend so effectively. She had to admit, she was interested. Maybe he was a stuffy suit, but he seemed like a thoughtful guy. There was a slight chance she'd agree to lunch sometime, if he dared ask again. She'd bitten his hand cleanly off the first time, but he'd shown admirable bravery twice.

"I think she'll love the scarf," she said in what she hoped was a professional tone. She placed some blue-and-pink plaid tissue in the bag and tried to arrange it like Haley would, but Summer's hands didn't quite work that way. She could sketch with the best of them and design amazing toys on her computer, but to make things look frou-frou was quite beyond her.

Chance extended his credit card. Summer couldn't resist touching his fingers again as she took the card. He focused the force of those teal-colored eyes on her. Summer had to grab on to the counter for stability. "Will that be all, sir?"

"Unless you know of a beautiful lady with honey-blonde hair who would be willing to go to dinner with me tonight?"

Smooth, real smooth. She tsked. "Hmm. Sorry, I don't. Jake down at the bar runs a high-dollar escort service. Check with him." Okay, so maybe she wasn't quite ready to say yes. It was too fun to tease with him.

Chance let out a laugh. "I generally try to avoid those."

"With your face I'm sure the women would pay you." Dang it! Had she just said that? She needed to stop fueling this man's ego. He obviously didn't need it. She handed him back the card and the slip to sign.

"Because I look like Channing Tatum?"

"Yeah, *that's* what I meant." Chance was a force all unto himself. She could see how he would be even more appealing than Channing Tatum, to her at least. She handed over the bag. "Well, good luck finding that woman."

"I think I'll need more than luck." He had the nerve to wink at her. Good for him.

"Probably," she agreed. "Those honey-blonde beauties can be pieces of work." He had called her beautiful. Not that she hadn't heard those words from a lot of men, but the validation from Chance warmed her. Though he'd also been confused why she'd be working as a clerk. *Join the club, buddy.*

He laughed again. "Maybe, but they're a lot of fun to be around." He winked once more and strode to the front door.

Summer watched him go. The view was nice and she liked the flirtations and banter, but she'd had her fill of suits who wanted her to settle down. She'd also had her fill of wanderers who only wanted a fling. Hmm. She wasn't sure where that left her. She'd have to see if there was a new category. Someone like MacKenzie's Isaac, a hard worker who didn't put airs on. Yet as she thought of Chance, it wasn't his lawyer persona that stood out. It was his fun, teasing manner and the fact that he looked as good in designer clothes as he had in bike shorts, and she hadn't thought anybody looked good in bike shorts before.

CHAPTER FOUR

CHANCE LOUNGED ON A BENCH ON MAIN STREET, WATCHING Summer lock the door of Sugar 'n' Spice. He'd found UPS and sent off Yvonne's gift, then went to lunch by himself, sitting in the sun and working on his laptop for a few hours at one of the outdoor tables on the back patio of the Sunflower Deli. He'd gotten Byron's latest requests accomplished, and Yvonne's as well. Everything was going well for Mumford's Sons; he just hoped he could keep Byron under control. Yvonne had been outraged when she found out Byron and Serena were dating. Byron kept claiming it was true love, but he'd been caught kissing the girl in his office less than three hours after Chance had talked to his brother. He sighed and shook his head, wishing Byron would find his true love and settle down. It would save his only brother a lot of stress.

As it got closer to five o'clock, he moved to a bench out front so he could keep an eye on Summer's shop door. He waited patiently, and close to six she appeared, locked the door, and retrieved a beach cruiser from the rack out front. He'd planned to follow her discreetly, until he found the right moment to casually talk to her, but he'd walked from his rental house. He didn't have a bike or a car, so he'd better approach her now.

Quickly stowing his computer in his bag and walking across Main Street, he touched her arm as she was bending over to unlock the bike.

"Whoa!" Summer jumped to her feet and faced him. "Hey. It's you." She smiled at him. It was a good smile, made her even more beautiful. "Did you find your honey-blonde hottie to go to lunch with?"

"Nope." He smiled. "Ate all by my lonesome, sadly."

"That is pathetically sad. Better luck with dinner." She wrapped the lock around the handlebars and clicked it.

"Does that mean you'll go with me?"

Summer arched back her head and shaded her eyes with her hand. Was it his imagination, or did she look like she wanted to say yes? "Naw. I have a strict no-dating-people-who-carry-around-laptops policy."

He pointed to the large leather purse slung over her shoulder. "You're carrying a laptop."

"And I'm not dating myself, am I?"

Chance laughed. He appreciated her smart-aleck attitude. "Who do I talk to if I want a written version of your policy? I'm sure I can find a loophole."

She considered him for a minute. "Sorry. The policy states that it can't be given out to anyone wearing a pressed shirt."

He smiled. "How about I pick up takeout, we go to my house, and I'll change my shirt?" But he could tell she didn't like the idea the second the words were out.

"*Way* too forward, lawyer boy. I still have Mace on me, even if I'm not running alone on a trail." She winked at him, and his entire body warmed.

"Okay, going back to my house is a bad idea."

"Bad reveal on your part." She started pushing the bike down the sidewalk, and he followed. "Now I know you're desperate for company *and* you're an over-the-top Richie. Most people would have a hotel room or maybe rent a condo for vacation. Not an entire house. It's too much. Especially for a single guy who can't get a date." She grinned at him.

Chance couldn't help but smile back, even though he didn't like her assumptions. "Something's wrong with having money?"

She glanced at him again, but then was distracted as they walked around an older couple. "I guess it depends what you do with that money."

"Spend it on you?" He was a bit rusty at the flirting and didn't have the funny responses up his sleeve that she seemed to have.

"Way wrong answer."

"Provide clothing, food, and work opportunities to refugees in Syria?" He had some worthwhile charities that he funded, and that was actually one of them.

"Hmm? I like it. Now you're getting somewhere."

They walked past Donita's Cantina, and delicious smells wafted out. His sandwich from the Sunflower Deli had been on the light side for him. "Can you smell that? It's like they're saying, 'Summer, you want to go to dinner with Channing Tatum's lookalike.'"

Summer laughed. "Hey, that's a vast improvement over 'Come back to my place and let's see if you *are* a call girl.'"

"Whoa! I never said anything like that. I'll have you know I'm a good Christian boy."

"Says every boy who wants a piece of my tush."

Chance couldn't help but laugh at that one, but the thought of any man trying to do what she was implying made him sick to his stomach. Maybe dinner wasn't such a good idea.

Summer stopped and placed a hand on his arm. Warmth rushed through him. "You okay?" she said. "Your face just went white."

"I don't like the thought of any man trying to proposition you."

"Including yourself?"

He held his hands up. "I promise that was not my intention. I simply wanted to get to know you better. You intrigue me, make me laugh, and you're the most beautiful woman I've ever seen."

Her eyebrows lifted. "Smooth, Judd, really smooth."

"Was it?" Her using his last name made him smile. He hadn't had anyone call him so many different nicknames in his life. His mom insisted on proper names and proper etiquette. He and his brother were ultra-successful, but their parents had been in the upper class before Mumford's Sons took off, his dad training them in investment capital from the time they were teenagers. His mom was a good lady, but she liked to show their status.

Summer smiled at him, and he knew he hadn't expressed fervently enough how drawn he was to her. He gave it one more shot. "Smooth enough you'll come eat some chips and guacamole with me?"

She moaned, and it did funny things to his stomach. Would she make a sound like that if he kissed her good and long? His eyes darted to her shapely lips, and he had to force himself to look away. *Slow down, Judd.*

"Why did you have to bring up guacamole when I'm starving? That's pretty low, mister."

He'd take any advantage he could get. "Fresh salsa, quesadillas, fajitas, carnitas, chimichangas."

"You had me at guacamole."

Chance laughed at the *Jerry Maguire* reference. "Good to know you're a simple girl."

"Only where food is concerned." She gave him a mischievous grin, and he had a hard time not swaying on his feet.

Chance took the bike from her loosened grip and pushed it onto the bike rack. She tilted her head and smiled at him, that soft-looking golden hair spilling over her toned shoulder.

"Guess I'm stopping here?" she asked.

"Yes, you are."

She nodded. "I don't mind a confident man, but there's a line, you know?"

Chance wasn't sure what that line was. He was definitely walking a tightrope with her and was in danger of falling into an abyss of honey-blonde hair and blue eyes. He wouldn't mind falling, not at all.

Chance placed his hand on Summer's lower back and escorted her through the open doorway and into the darkened hallway of the restaurant. Her breath shortened from the feel of those fingers—confident and warm—and she had to swallow hard. He was fun to tease and even more fun to stare at, but she needed to keep this to a casual dinner.

"Hello," Chance said to the hostess, who was dressed all in black. Her thick black makeup washed out her pale blonde hair and blue eyes. "Table for two, please."

The hostess held up two fingers, then pointed through the restaurant and walked away.

"Friendly, isn't she?" Chance murmured in Summer's ear, close enough that his lips brushed the sensitive skin of her lobe.

Summer's breath shortened, again. Okay, maybe a casual dinner wasn't a good idea if she couldn't even breathe being around him. "That was the warmest reception I've seen," she whispered back. "She must be a Channing Tatum fan too."

He chuckled and slid his hand from her lower back to her waist, pulling her in close like they were a couple or something. The lean muscle of his bicep brushed along her back and his body was firm and warm. It felt good, much too good.

"Hey, buddy." Summer stepped away and created some distance between them. "Casual dinner. No touchy-touch."

The hostess laid down menus and muttered, "Your waitress will be here shortly." Then she strode away.

Chance looked a little deflated by Summer's rejection. That had probably never happened before. She smiled to herself, though she would've liked to keep that arm around her waist. He held her chair out. She slid in and murmured, "Thank you." So he was a gentleman. Score one for Judd. Okay, he was scoring a lot higher than one already. She should've guessed a suit would be raised with good manners.

He sat, focusing on her instead of picking up the menu. "How long have you lived here?"

She bit her lip and opened her menu. "Two weeks."

A surprised laugh burst out. "You were giving me such a hard time, like you were born and raised in the valley."

She glanced back up. "Sorry. I always give strange men a hard time."

"I've known you two days now. I can't be considered strange anymore."

"True, but you're kind of fun to tease."

The waitress arrived with waters, a basket of chips, and a variety of salsas, then hurried off to get a mango lemonade for Chance and a Diet Coke for Summer.

"I didn't figure you for a pop kind of girl," Chance said.

"Why not?"

"Anyone who can run as fast as you usually would claim pop slows them down."

"Imagine how fast I'd be if I gave up my Diet Coke addiction." She winked. She actually didn't drink that much of her favorite pop anymore, trying to conserve her savings until she found a real job.

The waitress reappeared with their drinks and Summer took a long sip. Ah, fizzy-sweet heaven with that distinctive Coke bite.

"Do you need any recommendations?" the waitress asked with a friendly smile that more than made up for the hostess's cold reception.

Chance looked to Summer.

"I'm going to have the chimichangas," she said.

"Oh, you're ready to order already?" The waitress quickly flipped a pad of paper out.

"Oh, either way." Summer felt like she'd been too pushy and now she just felt awkward as she tried to explain. "I, um, it's just that I don't need any recommendations, because I had the chimichangas last time and they were fabulous."

The waitress smiled. "Great. Chicken or beef?"

"Chicken, please. And the black beans, and lots of guacamole."

"Got it." She turned to Chance, who was grinning at Summer.

"What?" Summer asked, defensively brushing her hair back over her shoulder.

"I've never seen you disconcerted."

"You've known me a total of fifteen minutes."

Chance chuckled. Summer had to focus on the waitress to avoid scooting her chair closer to his.

Chance turned to the waitress also. "I'll try whatever you recommend."

"Hmm?" The waitress appraised him. "I like this guy. Can you handle spicy?"

"Yes, ma'am."

The waitress laughed and took their menus. "Chili relleno with extra jalapeños it is." She walked away.

"You eat all those jalapeños and I'm not kissing you." Summer gasped. "I mean ..." Chance had focused those blue-green eyes on her and Summer literally lost her mind. At least that was her excuse.

He laughed and stood.

"Where are you going?" Summer stuttered, her face blazing hot.

"To chase down that waitress and tell her to forget the extra jalapeños. I'll change to a cheese quesadilla if necessary."

"Sit down." Summer grabbed his hand and tugged on it.

He willingly sat down, grinning at her and wrapping his fingers around her hand. "I didn't think I'd known you long enough to hold hands and talk about kissing, but I won't complain."

Summer wrenched her hand free and took a long drink of her Diet Coke, hoping it would calm down the heat in her face. Chance still hadn't wiped the smirk off his face. That dimple just wasn't fair. How was a girl supposed to deal with that?

He took a chip and dipped it in the salsa. "Is salsa okay, or is that going to ruin my chance for a kiss too?"

"Stop." Summer shook her head and laughed. "You were all looking at me, like, too deeply, and it just slipped out. Sorry."

"Don't apologize to me. This is a big step from you pulling Mace on me two days ago and telling me a few minutes ago, 'No touchy-touch.'"

"Sorry." She shook her head and took a chip too, breaking it in half and scooping up some salsa. "A girl has to be cautious."

"When she's as gorgeous as you, I'm sure she does."

Summer got caught up in his gaze and forgot she even had a chip in her hand. Salsa dripped over the side, running off her finger and onto the white tablecloth. "Oh. Oops." She popped the chip in her mouth and wiped her finger on her napkin. What was it about this man that had her acting like a complete dork? The spicy salsa couldn't be blamed for all the warmth in her face. "So, Mr. Judd. You're here in town for vacation and you're a lawyer. Where do you normally practice law?"

"Have we established that I am undeniably a lawyer?"

"You've just got that look."

"Aha." He loaded another chip with salsa. "Pegged by the look. What was it you called me, 'a suit'?"

"Well, if you've got the look, you have to own up to it. But you're dodging the question. Where do you hang your lawyer hat, Judd?"

"Charlotte."

"North Carolina? Hmm. That's why you talk all smooth and relaxed."

"I talk smooth and relaxed?"

He had no idea how smooth he talked. She grabbed another chip to not have to answer.

"What about you? You said you've only been here two weeks. Where did you move from?"

"I'm a wanderer. No home to speak of."

"Interesting." His eyes revealed he was interested, and she liked that a lot.

"You say interesting like it's a bad thing," she shot back.

"No. No. It's just ... interesting."

Summer cocked an eyebrow at him.

He cleared his throat. "Where is your favorite place to ... wander?"

"Anywhere warm, really." She sighed. It seemed like so long ago since she'd traveled with Taylor, though it'd only been a month. Like all her adventures were a happy dream she may never experience again. But that was dramatic thinking, and one thing Summer couldn't be accused of was being dramatic. "Have you been to Costa Rica?"

He shook his head.

"You're missing out, Mr. Suit. But Crested Butte is a good place to start unwinding and forgetting that you're all corporate and stuff. Maybe someday you can graduate to the Caribbean or Kauai."

"I have been to both. So why is Costa Rica so much better than Kauai or one of the other Caribbean islands?"

"Don't get me wrong, I'd never diss on Hawaii or the Caribbean, but Costa Rica is just unreal. The mountains, the forests, the beaches. Mountain biking there is to die for. They have a coastal trail from Las Catalinas that is fabulous, miles through quiet back country, views of the beach ..." Her voice trailed off as she realized he was staring at her, and not the *I'm enthralled by what you're saying* kind of stare. She tucked a lock of hair behind her ear and asked, "What?"

"'Those who *can't* run, bike'?" He arched an eyebrow. "Was that another honey-blonde beauty who said that to me?"

Her face was burning again. "I did say that." Oh, her flapping mouth.

"I think you owe me an explanation." He leaned back, folded his arms across his chest, and smirked.

Summer was momentarily distracted by the well-formed musculature of his biceps. She wanted to touch them and see if they felt as good as they looked. "You didn't get those from biking."

"Those?" His eyebrows arched up.

"Biceps," she clarified. Her face had no chance to cool down now.

Chance laughed. "I've been known to lift weights on occasion."

"'On occasion' meaning every day of the week?"

He smiled and shook his head. "Though I appreciate the compliment, you're evading my question. If you like to mountain bike so much, why don't you do it?"

Summer's hackles rose. "You could never understand my situation, Mr. Wealthy Pants, so don't even try."

The waitress approached their table with steaming plates of food. Summer took a sip of her Diet Coke, allowing Chance to thank the waitress. She cut a bite of the chimichanga and shoved it in. It burned the roof of her mouth. "Hot!" she gasped out, sucking in some air and taking a gulp of water with a mouth still full of food.

Chance regarded her like she was a bit off. He had every right to. She'd just chewed him out for being rich and not understanding, then she ate like she was a hick from Idaho or something. Chance hadn't touched his food. He stared at her and waited until she swallowed the bite before asking, "Can you please help me understand why you don't mountain bike?"

Summer studied her chimichanga and the lovely pile of guacamole next to it. Her throat filled with emotion, and she swallowed hard. She was not doing the pity party in front of Chance. Taking a long breath, she forced out the words, "I can't afford it anymore, okay?" She looked up at him and hoped her mask of indifference was in place. "It's fine.

Running is great. I still get to be out in nature." She took a chip and dipped it into the guacamole, shoving too large of a bite into her mouth. Her throat was still clogged with tears and she couldn't even figure out why she was being such a baby in front of Chance. She couldn't even enjoy the guacamole.

Chance was still staring at her. "I'm sorry, Summer," he finally said.

"No. Don't do that to me. I don't want your pity." She cleared her throat and was finally back in control of herself.

He nodded. "I understand. Do you want to tell me about it?"

She shrugged and cut away a smaller bite of her chimichanga, waiting for it to cool before plunging it into her mouth. It was really good now that she took the time to chew—warm cheese, spicy chicken, and some kind of creamy sauce that she fell instantly in love with. "Please, eat," she said to Chance.

He gave her a partial smile and took a bite of his chili relleno. He chewed slowly and then said, "That's got a good kick."

They ate in silence for a few minutes. Summer actually enjoyed the food and the quiet. She liked that they could just eat and not have to fill it with empty chatter.

Her chimichanga was about halfway gone and the guacamole was history when he asked again, "Will you tell me about it, Summer?"

She shrugged and twisted her cloth napkin between her fingers. "It's not that big of a deal." She looked down because it was a huge deal to her. "I'm a toy designer."

Chance looked at her approvingly. "Now that fits you much better than working at a home décor store."

She couldn't help but smile. "I love creating new toys. My dad owned an independent toy company. I started playing around with designing when I was young, like nine or ten."

"It's been your life passion."

"Yeah." She stirred her Diet Coke with the straw. "I went to Otis College of Art and Design in L.A. It's one of only two toy design schools in the nation, and within a year of graduation I was my dad's top designer."

"Good for you." His praise was warm and genuine. "What kind of toys do you specialize in?"

"Mostly classic ones made out of wood—puzzles, building toys, animals—but I also enjoy doing dolls. I created a line that's similar to the Polly Pockets, but my dolls are intricate and wooden, and the clothes are real cloth with buttons, zippers, and Velcro." She adored her Mini-Me dolls, but hated that they weren't hers any more. At his look of confusion, she smiled. "Polly Pockets are tiny plastic dolls with all kinds of interchangeable clothes and accessories."

"So your dad is a toy manufacturer or a toy store owner?"

"He was both. He had about a hundred retail stores where we sold our toys and all kinds of other toys as well, but we also manufactured and sold our trademarked toys throughout the world." Unable to look at him, she pushed the remaining black beans around on her plate. "He got bought out earlier this year. The new company owns my designs now, and they didn't want to manufacture anything new. They didn't want me." That sounded so pathetic. She knew it was more that they didn't want to pay her and they already had her designs, including the new Mini-Me line, which was one of the hottest toys of the year. What did they care if they had Summer? Yet she did an amazing job, she knew she did, and she prided herself on her new ideas. How could they just cut her and her family out?

Daring to look up, she saw that Chance's brow was pinched. He simply stared at her.

"So: long, sad story. No money, no traveling the world, no mountain biking." She shrugged. "It's fine, though. I'm still designing and I'll find someone great to work with soon."

Chance nodded shortly. "I'm sure you will. Did you like your dinner?"

Summer didn't know what to make of the rest of dinner. Chance was pleasant, but the playful banter was gone. He asked for her cell number before watching her ride off on Haley's beach cruiser. That was the only solid indicator that he cared enough to see her again. She wasn't sure where the evening had gone wrong. He seemed to approve of her career as a toy designer, but maybe it was just awkward for an extremely wealthy guy to figure out how to respond to someone that had fallen on hard times.

As soon as Summer had pedaled away, Chance dug his phone out of his pocket and jammed his finger against the touch screen, where Byron's name appeared as his most recent call. "The daughter's name was Gabriella, right?" he demanded.

"Excuse me?"

"Magical Dream Toys. The daughter was their top designer. What was her name?"

"Excuse me for me a second, Alyssa." Byron's voice was honey smooth.

"Alyssa! What happened to Serena?" Chance was already boiling with worry that Summer's story was going to coincide with his own. He couldn't handle Byron messing up with another secretary right now.

"Um, yeah. You were right about her, bro. Empty brain. She could drown in the shower."

Chance stormed down Main Street. He'd walked the mile into town and was glad now. He'd need at least that to calm down or he might break something in the rental house. "Byron, you are driving me nuts! Does Yvonne know?"

"She won't care. Serena is so dumb and needs the job, so she promised that she'd keep working and tell Yvonne that she broke up with me. Genius, eh? I can't wait for you to meet Alyssa. Her legs, whoa. I wish I could write poetry, you know?"

"Byron, you're a slimeball."

His brother chuckled. "What were you asking about the toy store deal?"

Dread settled in the pit of his stomach. If anything could make him forget about his brother's sleazy treatment of women, it was worrying if Summer was going to hate him. "What was the daughter's name? She didn't go by something different than Gabriella, did she?"

"Um, yeah, it was Gabriella."

Chance breathed again. It wasn't Summer, though the last name was the same. Could it actually be some crazy coincidence?

"But when I worked with Mr. Anderson to get a job for his son,

Jake, I asked if Gabriella needed a reference. He said she wanted to find a job on her own, but he called her something different, like a nickname for a free spirit. Let me think."

Oh no. Please, no.

"Sunrise or ... Summer! That was it, he called her Summer."

Chance halted and sank into an empty bench, his heart sinking deeper. He'd known it was her as soon as she told her story, but the stark reality about pulled him under. Was she going to hate him when she found out who he was? The daughter, Summer, had been traveling outside of the United States throughout the process of working with Magical Dream Toys and the takeover. She'd probably only heard of his company as Mumford's Sons. Her dad was the one Chance and Byron had dealt with.

"Oh, man." Chance pushed his hand into his forehead.

"What's going on? You okay?" Byron sounded genuinely concerned.

"You know the beautiful girl I met? Told you about a couple of days ago?" His brother had gone from one woman to the next in less time than he'd talked Summer into dinner. Unbelievable. Chance's entire time in Crested Butte had been caught up in daydreams of Summer.

"Oh, yeah. Glad to hear you finally broke the celibacy curse."

Chance shook his head. "She's Gabriella, or Summer, Anderson."

Silence scratched across the line. Finally, Byron muttered, "Aw, no. That's bad."

At least his brother got it. Chance stood and marched down the street again, pressing the phone hard into his ear and trying to control his panicked breathing. He finally found an amazing woman, and because of a business deal, he was going to lose her before they even had a chance.

"She doesn't know who you are?" Byron asked.

"She thinks I'm a lawyer. She knows my name, but it's possible she never heard our names, just Mumford's Sons."

"Okay. It's all okay, then. Just don't tell her."

"'Don't tell her'? You want me to lie?" Chance exploded, earning a nasty glare from an elderly woman walking the other direction. "Sorry," he whispered to her.

"You *always* tell the truth, young man," she admonished.

Chance nodded meekly. "Yes, ma'am."

"Humph." She shook her head and stomped off, muttering about young people.

Chance blew out his breath and kept walking, but slowed his pace a little bit—he didn't need to run over tourists or be rude. "I just got chewed out by an old lady."

Byron laughed so loud it rattled Chance even further. "You're such a boy scout, bro. If Summer doesn't connect the dots, why do you need to do it for her?"

"Because that's what us boy scouts do."

"Come on! Work with me here. Oh, sorry, Alyssa. No, it's not another girl." Byron sighed loudly. "Can you please say hi to Alyssa?"

Chance didn't have a second to say no. He couldn't care less if Alyssa realized his brother was a two-timing jerk and wouldn't stay loyal to her if she *was* his soul mate.

"Hi," a sultry voice said.

"Hi, Alyssa." He didn't inject any emotion into his voice. "Can I please talk to my brother now?"

"Sheesh. I'm glad I got the fun one."

There was giggling and laughter and a scuffle for the phone. Byron came back on, panting. "I gotta go, bro. Lie to her—it's the only way for you."

"You wouldn't lie to me," Alyssa protested so loudly Chance could hear.

"Of course not, baby, but I couldn't lie to you. Not with the connection we have between us." The phone disconnected, and Chance was relieved. He didn't want to hear the crap his brother would spew to keep on kissing something pretty. How were they even related?

He stowed his phone and slowed his steps as he walked through the park east of town. What was he going to do? He'd never taken his brother's advice where women were concerned, but he was tempted. Groaning, he shoved a hand through his hair. He couldn't lie, especially not to Summer. But if he told her the truth, they'd be over before they began. Maybe he could just postpone telling her everything. If she never asked what his company was called, why would he needlessly volunteer up the information? That would be awkward, right?

He rolled his eyes at himself. He was justifying, like Byron would do. No, Byron wouldn't justify or lie; he prided himself on his honesty. He'd tell the woman the truth, but be so charming about it she'd forgive him and be kissing him by sunset. It wasn't fair that Byron could enchant and beguile any woman who looked his direction.

Chance shuffled through the park and on the road out toward his rental house. He didn't know what to do, but he had to get to know Summer. He'd finally broken through her wall of not wanting to date him, and he couldn't give up now. She was too refreshing and beautiful and funny, too much of everything he'd always wanted to find in a woman. He wouldn't lie to her, but he had to give them a chance before he spilled the truth. Just a few days, and hopefully she'd be interested in him before he dropped the bombshell that might kill any chance he had.

CHAPTER FIVE

THE NEXT DAY, WHEN SUMMER EXITED THE STORE, CHANCE WAS standing on the sidewalk, grinning at her.

She was hard-pressed to hide a smile of her own. "You just going to wait for me every day after work, cowboy?"

"I'd like to make it a standing date."

Summer liked the idea and the way he looked at her, not leering, but definitely appreciative. She'd had a good time with him yesterday. He seemed like a stand-up guy, and how could she turn down Channing Tatum's lookalike? "You wait there, wearing that dimple, and I might be persuaded."

He'd laughed and she went to dinner with him that night. He was there every night after that, even when it rained and all she would've had to look forward to was a miserable ride home and macaroni and cheese. For two weeks she teased him each time she opened the shop door and found him waiting, but he always talked Summer into dinner. Not that he had to talk too hard. She liked being around him more and more every day. Sometimes he got a little distant or looked at her like he knew something she should know, but most of the time they laughed, talked, and enjoyed simply being together. She appreciated that he didn't ask for more than dinner. At this point in her life, if a guy was going to have a chance, he needed to get to know her and move at a snail's pace.

Friday night was a gorgeous summer evening in Crested Butte, and Summer hoped if Chance took her to dinner they could sit out on a patio and enjoy this weather. When she opened the door, her handsome "standing date" stood outside with a picnic basket hooked through one arm.

"Hey," Summer said, locking up the door quickly and turning to him. "Somebody's trying to be a little original."

"Trying." Chance chuckled. "I'd love to plan something original, but when I met my honey-blonde beauty she told me to 'try again in two weeks.' It's been over two weeks since I ran you off the trail."

Summer unlocked her bike and started to stroll next to him, liking how comfortable she was with him already. "So what does that mean to me, Mister?"

"Guess you'll see tomorrow when I plan a really original date."

"Yeah?" She tilted her head and studied him.

"Yeah." His teal eyes twinkled. "Picnic in the park work for tonight?"

"Perfect. How'd you know I'd want to be outside?"

"I'm getting to know you pretty well."

"You wish."

Chance chuckled.

They made their way slowly east, smiling at little children and walking side by side until they reached the park. Chance whipped a blanket out of his basket and proceeded to unload hoagie sandwiches, fruit, cookies, and water bottles. The park was perfect tonight, probably in the high seventies, which was sweltering for Crested Butte even in the summer. Children ran, climbed, and giggled on the playground, and some teenage boys were tossing a Frisbee with upbeat music thumping from their portable speakers.

"So does the fancy attorney just order someone to do all of this for him, or are you bored here on vacation and that's why you seek me out every day?"

"Two loaded questions there." Chance leaned back on an elbow, stretched out his legs, and popped a grape in his mouth.

Summer threw a grape at him. "Answer both."

He chuckled. "Yes, my assistant called around and the basket was delivered. No, I'm not bored; my brother and assistant have plenty of work for me to do. I barely get out for a ride each morning, searching for a beautiful runner every time and not finding her."

"I make sure to go on the trails that bikers can't use." She stood and bowed to him.

Chance grabbed her hand and tugged her back down. She stumbled right on top of him. Everything seemed to slow down. His warm body felt wonderful underneath her, and his dimple deepened as he grinned slowly at her.

"You didn't answer the second question to my satisfaction," Summer murmured, trying not to notice how nice his lips were shaped.

"Hmm?" His eyes darted to her lips, and Summer felt herself being drawn in by his strong arms.

"Do you only come find *me* every night because you're bored?"

"I'm definitely not bored. You're the only person I want to find every night." He clamped his hands around her lower back. She had no escape, and she loved it.

Whack! Summer was hit in the head by a Frisbee, and she learned that the term "seeing stars" was not facetious. Chance's arms loosened. Rolling off of him onto the blanket, she grasped at her forehead and winced.

"Summer! You okay?" Chance sat up.

"Sorry," she heard a young male voice squeak from above. "Is she okay?"

"I'm fine," Summer muttered. She opened her eyes to see Chance peering down at her and two teenage boys haloed above him by the sun. "Nice shot."

The boys gave surprised laughs, and Chance's eyes widened.

"I'm sorry," the dark-haired boy repeated. "I didn't mean to hit you."

"He sucks at Frisbee," the blond with long shaggy hair explained.

"No worries. I always throw it the wrong direction too."

Chance offered a hand and she sat up, her head clearing quickly. The boys still watched her with concern.

"I promise. I'm fine. No worries."

The blond looked at Chance. "You've got a really chill girlfriend."

Chance nodded. "Thanks."

"Sorry," they both said again. They shuffled away, but Summer heard the dark-haired kid add, "And a freaking hot girlfriend too."

Chance grinned with a teasing lilt to his lips.

"You do *not* have a hot girlfriend," Summer said. "Unless there's someone you aren't telling me about."

"I wish I could claim you."

Summer bit at her lip. The worst part about the Frisbee attack was the interruption of a possible kiss. Chance was reeling her in faster than her dad could cast a fly and snag a trout.

He eyed her with too much concern. "You're sure you're okay? You have a little mark right here." He gently touched her forehead.

Summer smiled. "It's good." She took a bite out of her sandwich and a swallow of her water to prove she was fine. "I'm not that fragile."

He arched his eyebrows. "That's good to know. Now that I've got the go-ahead to plan original dates and everything."

"I'm looking forward to that," Summer said.

"I Will Wait" by Mumford & Sons started playing on the speakers her Frisbee buddies had set up.

"I love this song." Summer climbed to her feet and started dancing, further ready to show Chance that she was okay, even if her head throbbed a little bit.

Chance watched her for a few seconds with an amused grin.

Summer reached out a hand. "Dance with me?"

He climbed up quickly, took her hand, and swayed with her, singing the chorus in this sexy, low voice: "And I will wait, I will wait for you."

When the banjo picked up, he swung her out, then in. Summer laughed, but she actually felt like Chance *would* wait for her. But what were they both waiting for? Her to find a job? His vacation to be over and their relationship to either fizzle or go to the next level? Summer didn't know, but after two weeks of learning to trust him and fully enjoying being around him, she was ready to see what the possibilities were.

Chance watched Summer pedal away on her bike and cursed Frisbee throwers the world over. She had wanted to kiss him. He knew it. He'd been trying to take things slow, though his male instincts had been begging him to speed things up. The teenaged Frisbee throwers had been dead on about Summer. She was unbelievably hot and chill at the same time—funny, smart, laid-back, and with more world experiences than he'd imagined—Summer may just be the perfect woman for him. Now if only he could convince her of that and somehow bring up the fact that he was Mumford's Sons. He groaned, hoping his face hadn't betrayed his worries when the band Mumford & Sons had come on and she'd danced so cute.

Holding her in his arms was heaven, and as soon as she found out who he was, he'd be thrust out of any hope of paradise. She was going to hate him.

CHAPTER SIX

SUMMER'S PHONE RANG AS SHE WAS GETTING HOME FROM HER morning hike to the top of the ski resort. She couldn't help but smile that it was Chance. This was the first time he'd called her, and she hoped whatever he wanted to do tonight was that step she'd decided last night she wanted to take.

"Hey," she said.

"Hi, Summer." Just the way he said her name made her a little breathless. "Are you working today?" he asked.

"I'm scheduled to go in from noon to close, as always." Hmm. He wanted a day date, did he?

"Oh. I was hoping you might have Saturday off. Can you find someone to work for you?"

"Why should I?" She leaned into a hamstring stretch and smiled to herself. He was so fun to tease.

"If you don't, you'll miss out on the fun day I have planned for you."

"Oh, really? Who says it'll be fun? Lawyers have a different version of fun than toy designers." Straightening, she lowered her heels off her porch to stretch her calves.

"I think I've got a bead on what a certain honey-blonde beautiful toy designer would think of as fun."

She bit at her lip, thinking it would be fun to kiss him. "Let me see what I can do about work."

"Okay. Call me back."

He disconnected and she stayed in the hamstring stretch, smiling to herself.

"Haven't seen a smile like that on you since you came to stay." Haley and Isaac's dad, Trevor, stood next to her front porch, smirking at her. "What's his name?"

"Chance," she said before she could stop herself.

Trevor's face broke into a grin. "Hmm. You're going to take a *chance*, are you?"

"Very funny."

"Well, I expect to meet that young man before you go off smooching him, you hear?"

"Let's get something straight, Papa Turnbow. Just because I'm living off your goodwill doesn't mean you get to harass my boy toys." Summer grinned at him. She really liked her friends' dad.

"Ha!" Trevor chortled. "I can harass whoever I want if they come on my property."

"I'll make sure I meet him somewhere else, then." She winked obnoxiously.

Trevor's scowl was fierce. "Now, we aren't having any of that. He'd better treat you good, get your door, walk you to the porch, and all that, or I really will pull out my old pals Smith and Wesson. They served me well when Haley was growing up, and when MacKenzie stayed here last summer."

"Got it." Summer laughed and shook her head.

"You bride pact friends always give me something to smile about."

"Glad to be of service, sir."

Trevor walked off, grinning. Summer was glad she was here. It seemed Trevor was as lonely for fun interaction as she was.

Summer pushed MacKenzie's number. "Hey, friend, can you work for me this afternoon?"

"For sure. You haven't taken an afternoon off the entire month you've been here."

"I need the money," Summer muttered, brought back to her sad reality.

"Hey, you'll find an awesome company soon and be rocking it before you know it."

"Thanks."

"Are you doing something fun?"

"I don't know what we're doing."

"We?"

"I've got a date." She let out a little squeal.

MacKenzie laughed. "Sounds like he's a cute one."

"Oh yes, he looks like Channing Tatum, but cuter." She hated that she lived a few miles from her friend but never saw her. She'd been going to dinner with Chance for two weeks and the only girl friend she'd bragged to was Taylor, and that was just a quick text conversation because Taylor was off touring Thailand.

"Whoa. I think the only man I know cuter than Channing Tatum is Isaac."

Summer laughed. "You would."

"Plan on me this afternoon, and I want an update on the date. Be safe, 'kay?"

"Don't worry. I always carry my old pal, Mace." She smiled, thinking how Chance would react if Trevor actually pulled out his old pals Smith and Wesson. Now that would make for a good laugh.

"Good girl. Talk to you soon." MacKenzie hung up.

Summer called Chance back. "I'm in."

"Glad to hear it."

"What should I wear?"

"Do you have any biking shorts?"

"Chance," she breathed. "You didn't."

"Yes, I did. I'll be there in a few minutes."

Summer hung up the phone and held it to her chest. Chance was taking her on a bike ride. She jumped onto the porch with another squeal, a bit louder this time, pushed through the front door, and ran to her bedroom. She needed to shower off the running sweat and get ready for biking sweat. Yes!

Chance drove into a well-kept ranch yard. Summer had texted him this address. She was finally confiding in him where she lived. It was close to where he wanted to take her on the ride, so it worked out great. She'd told him to go straight to the smaller house, as the guy in the bigger house would probably give him a hard time. He smiled. She cared if someone gave him a hard time. He'd felt conflicted over the past two weeks not telling her who he really was, but he put those issues from his mind. He was going to enjoy the day, and soon he would tell her the truth.

She opened the door and his resolve to not ever tell her the truth wavered. She was so beautiful, and when she looked at him with those blue eyes, they were filled with trust. Like she thought he was a great guy and would take good care of her. He really would, yet he was hiding something huge from her and it gnawed at him.

"You ready to go?" he asked.

Summer flung herself at him and gave him a tight hug. Chance took the hug willingly, wrapping his arms around her fit frame. She pulled back, but he wasn't ready to release her yet. He loved her spontaneity. He'd been afraid she wouldn't want him spending money on her, but her natural exuberance and desire to ride bikes seemed to win out.

"Thank you!" she gushed. "I'm so excited I could just hug anybody."

Chance's arms dropped away then. "Oh, so you didn't want to hug me, I was just the only person around?"

"I already hugged Trevor, so I figured you deserved one too."

"Trevor?" Jealous darts fired in his gut. Who was Trevor, and how was Chance going to push the guy out of the picture? She'd said nothing about Trevor at any of their dinner dates.

Summer smiled coyly and tilted her head to the side. Her long hair spilled over her tanned shoulder.

Chance couldn't resist trailing his fingers through her hair, then gripping her shoulder lightly. "Who is Trevor?"

She giggled. "My friend, Haley's, dad."

Haley's dad. She had told him about the older man, but called him

Papa Turnbow. Chance forced himself to release her shoulder and smile at her. "Got to tease me every chance you get."

She clucked her tongue. "I like seeing that jealous light in your eyes."

"Do you, now?" He took a step closer.

She held her ground and grinned up at him. "Oh, yeah. It's pretty cute."

"Yeah?" He took another step and their bodies were inches apart. Feeling all kinds of brave because she wanted him to be jealous and she'd basically said he was cute, he wrapped his arms around her back again and pulled her flush against him. "You're pretty cute, but I wouldn't try to make you jealous."

Her breath was coming in short pants as she gazed up at him, her blue eyes luring him in. "You're just a better person than me."

All romantic thoughts fled. Chance swallowed and released his hold on her. He wasn't a better person. He was lying to her and felt partially responsible for her situation. Her eyes filled with confusion, but he couldn't fill in the gaps. Couldn't or wouldn't? It was still too early to tell her about their awful connection.

"You ready to go?" he asked.

"Yeah. Let me grab my backpack." She hurried back into the house, returning a few seconds later with a small backpack and two water bottles.

"You are prepared." He tried to tease and lighten the mood again. For once in his life he wished he was more like Byron. His brother would've taken that kiss and then some, and not felt guilty for one second about taking advantage of the most amazing woman Chance had ever met.

"Even got my Mace packed in here." She held the bag aloft and grinned at him. Her sparkling expression was back, and he hoped she didn't wonder what in the world was wrong with him, backing away like that. Dumb conscience anyway.

"Oh, good." He laughed uneasily. "You might need that." Honestly, a shot of Mace would probably feel better than the guilt that was consuming him right now.

She laughed and walked in front of him to his rented Land Rover, pausing to look over the bikes on the rack. "You rented us Yetis?"

She knew her bikes. He shouldn't be surprised. "Um, no. I bought these."

"Oh." She glanced down at the ground, then kind of squeaked out, "I don't want you buying anything for me."

Chance would gladly give her the bikes if she wanted them, especially with how guilty he was feeling about his role in her losing her job and designs, and by extension her ability to buy a Yeti for herself. "I bought them when I flew into Gunnison a few weeks ago. I like to have two in case I have trouble with one."

"Oh." Her smile reappeared. "Oh, good. I'm okay with being your backup bike rider."

He chuckled. He liked her far too much. He wanted to wrap his arms around her and tell her she was much more than backup to him or something cheesy like that, but he refrained and opened her door. Hopefully his guilt wouldn't override his good sense and they could have a fabulous day together.

Chance parked his Land Rover in a dirt parking lot near the Judd River Falls trailhead, a few miles past Crested Butte.

"Hey, I just realized one of my favorite hiking trails is named after you," Summer teased.

Chance grinned. "Favorite trail for your favorite guy?"

"You wish. So, where are we biking?" Summer changed the subject quickly. She was a little hurt and confused why Chance had backed away when she would've kissed him on her front porch. It had happened a few times. She'd say something and he'd get a little weird. She wasn't quite sure what to think about that. Should she be concerned or just give him space?

"Are you up for an adventure?" he asked.

"Sure."

"A tough climbing adventure that will leave us needing a hot tub at the end of the day?"

"Bring it on." Her excitement mounted. She hadn't had an adventure like she used to experience all the time with her closest friend from Camp Wallakee, Taylor, for too long. Was he going to take her to a hot tub after? Hmm. She didn't mind the thought of seeing Chance in a suit. As shredded as his arms and calves were, she imagined his chest would be more than drool-worthy.

"Have you heard of the Pearl Pass Bike Tour?" The man himself interrupted her daydreams about him.

Her eyes widened. "Where they ride from Crested Butte to Aspen?"

He nodded.

"Yes! I've always wanted to do that." She did a little dance and almost threw herself into his arms again. Doing crazy adventures that most people only talked about doing was her favorite pastime.

"Nice dance." He grinned. "Are you okay if I have you back by tomorrow morning?"

Summer's breath caught. Crap. He was going to push her, and she hated that. She tilted her head and gave him a challenging look. "As long as we've got separate rooms, big boy."

"We do."

The moment went slow and sticky as they stared at each other. Chance was going to be a gentleman, and he was accepting her terms. She hoped he knew what this meant for her to trust him enough to stay the night, even if it was in separate rooms.

He cleared his throat and broke the spell. "We're not doing the whole route as they start a few miles back in Crested Butte, but I think it'll be close enough for us."

"Yay us!"

Chance chuckled. He pulled a bike off the rack and held it next to her. "I'm not a professional at adjusting these, but I can get it pretty close."

"No worries. I'm a professional rider, so I can deal with it not being perfect."

He laughed again and got busy adjusting the bike. When Summer climbed on, she smiled. "It's perfect. Race you to the top."

"You gotta give me a head start, Ms. Professional Bike Rider."

Chance grabbed his bike and secured his water bottles, then swung his backpack on.

Summer was excited about the challenge. She hadn't been on a bike for a while and hoped she didn't keel over climbing to the top of the pass, but she'd make it somehow, especially after she'd just bragged about being a professional.

The first couple of miles were pretty gradual and they could ride side by side and chat. It was pleasant with the sun shining and the air a perfect seventy degrees, but then the climb really started and the trail became single file. Summer insisted he lead the way and set the pace. Within minutes, she had no breath left to talk as her legs burned. She had no clue how far they'd gone, it felt like hours had passed, when Chance called over his shoulder, "Let's take a break."

"Hallelujah," Summer muttered, stopping her bike and reaching for her water bottle.

"How are you feeling?" Chance propped his bike against a tree and walked back to her, taking her bike so she could stretch her shoulders.

"Humiliated."

"What? Why?"

"I bragged about being a professional. I used to be able to bike and keep up with anyone. Tragically, I haven't been on a bike in months and I am feeling it."

Chance chuckled. "You're doing great. I don't feel like I'm slowing down at all and I bike at least once a week."

"Thanks." She wasn't sure if he was being placating or not, but she'd take it. "Are we there yet?" She put a little whine in her voice.

He smiled. "I think we're about halfway through the climb; then it's all downhill from there. Rough downhill, but still easier than this. Are you hungry?"

"Famished," she said dramatically, but truly her stomach was the least of her worries. She'd eat because it would give her energy and give her legs a break. Taking her pack off her back, she pulled out an apple. Chance propped her bike up against a tree and they sat on boulders as they shared his Luna bars and her apple. It felt intimate to be sharing a piece of fruit. Weird, but nice.

This bike ride reminded her of her favorite excursion through

Costa Rica. She'd been with Jerome then, but she didn't even miss him. She'd traveled through many countries, usually with a different boyfriend, but she hadn't felt the connection to a man like she did with Chance. No matter how many times she tried to tease him and step away, he kept coming back, and she liked it.

"Thanks for planning this day. You're a thoughtful guy."

He kicked at a rock. "I try."

"So, tell me something about Chance Judd. How do I know nothing about your family? I thought we were tighter than that." Weird that family hadn't come up the past two weeks at dinner, but they'd mostly talked about traveling and she'd shared a lot about her girl's camp friends who lived in the valley, and of course Taylor, who she loved like a sister.

He glanced up at her and gave her that smile and irresistible dimple. She wanted to touch it. "Just the usual. Two parents. Older brother."

She nudged her shoulder with his. "Hey, what do you know? I'm the usual two parents and one older brother too. I do have a little sister to add to the mix."

"I would've liked a little sister. What's she like?"

"Stinking cute and one of those take-on-the-world kind of girls. Kennedy's just finishing up college, but then it's going to be like, look out, here comes the first woman President of the United States."

He grinned. "Good for her. You're a take-on-the-world kind of girl too. Your parents must've done something right."

She felt herself go red. It was nice he thought that of her, but right now she felt like she was at a stalemate. If she didn't find a new employer soon, she might go nuts. She needed to create, not just the plans, but seeing it through to a product that was going to bring a smile to a child. If only she could afford to manufacture her designs, or get humble enough to ask her father for a loan and his manufacturing contacts.

"Thank you kindly, sir," she said, very smart-alecky so he wouldn't know she was giving in to depressing thoughts. "So, what's your brother like? Mine's stuffy and boring. Nice enough guy, but a total suit, so we don't need to talk about him."

"Definitely don't like those suits." He winked, then crumpled up the Luna bar wrappers in his hand. "My brother's a real pain. Loves women and making money. In that order."

"Whoa." She didn't like his brother already. "Sounds like a real charmer."

Chance studied the ground and rolled a pebble around under his biking shoe. "To the women he's after, I'm sure he is." He sighed. "He actually is charming. Everyone likes him, and he does good stuff too. He's always finding a new charity to donate to, though most of the time it's because the woman he's currently dating is into that charity. He's my business partner and he's really smart and hard-working, honest, always watches out for people."

"Good qualities. So why'd you turn out so different?"

"What do you mean?" He focused those blue-green eyes on her.

"You don't seem like a womanizer or someone who's caught up in money, even though you obviously have plenty."

He shrugged. "I'd rather have one fabulous woman than a hundred empty-headed ones." His gaze was burning into her now.

Summer had a bike helmet and funny-looking bike shorts on and probably stunk like sweat, but she'd never been so tempted to initiate a first kiss. Chance leaned toward her, and she moistened her lips and wished she had a breath mint. He lifted his hand and brushed at her mouth. "You had a Luna bar crumb."

Summer laughed self-consciously and glanced down. When she looked back up, Chance was studying her. She didn't know if he was going to make a move or not, and the silence was getting to be a bit much for her. "Have you found that one fabulous woman yet?"

He smiled. "I'm getting there."

Summer grinned at him.

He stood and offered her a hand up. Summer felt a sudden chill. Was it the sweat cooling on her skin, or the fact that Chance could've kissed her again, but hadn't? He either had the self-control of Captain America or he wasn't into her. Dang on both.

They climbed back onto their bikes and she noticed he set a slower pace up the grueling trail. She appreciated that, and him taking the lead. If she would've been up front, she would've killed herself trying to prove that she was strong, even though she'd admitted to him that she was out of biking shape.

A couple hours later, they were above the tree line, riding in the scree. They'd actually had to get off their bikes and hike for a bit to the false summit, but now the real summit was in sight. Her legs screamed in pain.

"Can I walk my bike the rest of the way up?" she called to Chance.

He turned back. "Sure, if I can. My legs are about to fall off."

Chance's tire slipped on the unstable rocky trail, and before she could do anything but scream out, his bike had flipped out from under him and he hit the rocks with his elbows and knees.

Summer jumped from her bike, dropping it and wincing as the twelve-thousand-dollar bike hit the rocks, but she had to get to Chance. She reached him in a couple of steps. He rolled over with a groan.

"Are you okay?" she rasped out.

"Yeah."

"Where does it hurt?" Her eyes scanned his body. There were some scrapes on his elbows and knees, a bit of blood, but nothing too gory or dripping.

Chance sat up and shook his head. "Just some road rash. It's okay."

"I think it'd be rock rash." She tried to smile, but it was shaky. Seeing him go down had unnerved her. She hadn't realized she was that invested in him and keeping him safe.

He chuckled. "Did I really just crash while we were going five miles per hour?"

"You're going to be in trouble on the downhill."

"Seriously." He brushed at some rocks embedded in his knees.

"Don't. Wait." Summer sat on the rocky ground next to him and pulled off her backpack. She retrieved a packet with some sterile wipes and bandages and set to work cleaning his wounds and putting Band-Aids on anything that was bleeding.

Chance simply watched her as she worked, his stare unnerving. She felt like she was in some Nicholas Sparks' book with Channing Tatum giving her his smoldering gaze. But this was Chance, and he was real and even more appealing to her than the serious-looking star.

"All better," she said, pasting on a brave smile and shoving the garbage into a separate pocket of her backpack.

Chance didn't move, still studying her. "You're pretty amazing, you know that?"

Summer lifted her hands. "I'm here to serve."

He chuckled, then unbuckled her bike helmet, set it next to her, and gently cupped her chin with his palm. "I'll take you as my nurse any day."

It was one of the few times in her life that Summer had nothing to say. He drew her in closer with his hand, leaning down to meet her. Their lips connected and warm currents rushed through her. Summer shifted closer to him, returning his kiss with a fervency she hadn't felt in a while. Chance wrapped both hands around her waist and easily lifted her onto his lap. Summer gasped, and he smiled, then cradled her in his arms and proceeded to kiss her until she was breathless and wanting more.

"Coming through!" a voice called from below them on the trail.

Summer jumped, scrambling to her feet. Chance climbed up behind her and they stepped out of the way.

A couple of college-aged kids rode past, grinning at them. "I'd make out in the trees next time," one of them said.

Chance turned to her as the boys continued up the trail. "I'd take a kiss from you wherever I could get it."

Summer self-consciously brushed her ponytail behind her shoulder. "I didn't figure the first kiss would be with you wearing a bike helmet and me sweaty and gross."

"You're not gross, but I'll work on my romantic spots tonight."

"Sounds good."

Chance smiled before bending down and examining his bike. "Just a few scratches. More than worth that kiss."

"You scratched up a Yeti and think a kiss is worth that?"

"You're worth much more than a Yeti."

Summer beamed, feeling like in his eyes she really was.

Chance whistled as he shaved for the night. The ride down the mountain had been exhilarating, if a bit dangerous in a few spots. They'd laughed a lot, and he'd been reminded how much he loved Summer's zest for life. Luckily, neither of them had wrecked again. When he showered and examined his earlier road rash, none of it was deep and he was able to throw away the bandages Summer had so carefully applied. He smiled, thinking about her doctoring him up so tenderly, and that kiss ... whew. He couldn't wait for tonight.

Summer had teased him about being a spoiled rich kid, but also claimed to be impressed when the St. Regis Hotel had picked them up at the bottom of the trail. The hotel staff took care of their bikes, planning to ship them back to Crested Butte. Chance and Summer were whisked to their rooms, where refreshment, clothes, and toiletries were waiting.

He'd have to send Yvonne more than a scarf as a thank-you for coordinating all of this. He dressed quickly in navy slacks and a button-down off-white shirt, wondering if it was too quick to knock on Summer's door. Today had been a fun adventure, but the best part was being with her. She'd made him forget about the worries over her finding out his part in the sale of her dad's company. She made him laugh more than anyone he'd ever been with. Summer was so great, maybe she'd forgive him when she found out the truth. Maybe. He frowned at his reflection, brushing some gel through his short hair and spraying some Grey Vetiver on his neck.

His phone beeped with an incoming text. Yvonne.

You made it to Aspen yet?

Yes, and I owe you. Thanks for setting all this up.

You're really going to think you owe me when you see the dress and swimsuit I got your girl. Can't wait to hear all about it.

Now I can't wait to go get her. Thanks.

I accept money, jewelry, and chocolate as payment.

I'm on it!

Chance smiled, pocketed his wallet, phone, and key card, and strode out his suite door, more than anxious to see the dress Yvonne had mentioned on Summer. She usually dressed pretty casually, in a T-shirt and flowing, knee-length skirts. Swimsuit? Oh, yeah. Hopefully he'd get to see that suit later. His legs and back would love a stop at the hot tub after dinner, but he'd be happy to do whatever Summer wanted.

Summer's suite was just across the hall from his. He rapped softly on the door. She swung it open, and her eyes went up and down, then focused on his face. "You clean up nicely."

Chance's mouth was hanging half open. "Um, you ..." He gestured to the long, gorgeous hair curling down her back, and the red dress clinging to all her curves. It was sleeveless with a V-neck that was deep enough to make his throat dry, but still classy. The dress more than flattered her. Yvonne was getting gifts *and* another raise. "You're gorgeous," he managed to say.

She rolled her eyes. "I don't even have makeup on. Dang man getting ready too fast."

His eyes swept over her smooth skin, shapely lips, and blue eyes. "You don't need makeup."

She stuck her tongue out and laughed. "Says the man who's starving, right? I'll be two minutes."

She swept back to the bathroom, and Chance was left staring. He was starving, but food wasn't on the top of the list for what he needed. He settled on the couch to wait, deleting emails to distract himself.

True to her word, she was back within minutes. Chance stood, and he was sure his tongue was lolling out of his mouth. "You look amazing."

"See, the makeup helps." She fluttered her long, darkened eyelashes and tucked a strand of hair behind her ear.

"You don't need makeup to be gorgeous."

She smiled and took his arm. "Thank you for all of this." She gestured to her dress, then the room. "How did you know what size I am?"

"I have a really amazing assistant."

"And?" She grabbed a scarf thing off the chair, and he helped her wrap it around her shoulders. When his fingers grazed her bare skin, a fire started in the pit of his stomach.

He cleared his throat and stepped back, even though he really wanted to kiss her again. "I sent her a picture of you."

"How do you have a picture of me?"

"I'm sneaky like that."

"Scary sneaky." She grinned. "So, what are we eating? Are you starving? That ride and surviving on Luna bars about killed me, but the fruit, cheese, crackers, and water helped." She pointed at the bar. "This is unreal. Do you live like this all the time?"

Chance didn't know what else to do but shrug. His penthouse in uptown Charlotte was much nicer and ten times bigger than either of these suites, and he had catered food delivered every day. Was she nervous being with him tonight? She didn't usually rattle on like that.

"I'm starving too," he said. "Do you like sushi?"

"Love it."

Chance couldn't resist squeezing the delicate hand resting on his arm. He'd found the perfect woman. If only he wasn't also responsible for her family selling their business and her losing her job and designs. He pushed the thought out of his mind. Tonight was about enjoying Summer. Maybe tomorrow he'd get brave and spill the truth.

CHAPTER SEVEN

SUMMER FELT LIKE ROYALTY AS CHANCE ESCORTED HER DOWN THE
elevator and out into the summer night. It was high-elevation
Colorado, so not balmy, but a nice low-seventies. She wouldn't
complain, and especially not about spending more time with the hunk
next to her. He looked like every woman's dream man with the
sculpted face, blue-green eyes, and that irresistible dimple when he
smiled at her. His button-down shirt and dress pants flattered his
frame nicely. Yummy.

The restaurant was just down the block from the hotel, so they
were there in minutes and opted to sit out on the patio. The waiter
was quick to bring water, and they were both so hungry they immedi-
ately ordered edamame and a shrimp tempura roll to start. Summer
perused the menu, but found her eyes drawn back to Chance.

"What?" He grinned.

She couldn't resist pressing her index finger into his dimple. "I love
that thing," she whispered.

Chance grasped her finger before she could pull back and pressed a
kiss on its tip.

Summer's mouth went dry. "What do you say we skip dinner and go
make out?" she asked.

Chance's eyebrows shot up and he laughed, loud and long. He stopped long enough to take a drink of water and pinned her with a look. "Do you just say whatever comes into your mind?"

"Yes, sir." She glanced back at her menu, embarrassed that she really had said that. "I was just kidding, though. I really am hungry."

"Okay." He sighed dramatically. "After dinner, though?" He reached over and squeezed her hand.

"Plan on it," she murmured, thrills racing through her body. She should probably find a way to slow down this romance train, but she had no desire to.

Dinner passed quickly—the sushi, garlic shrimp, and baby back ribs were all delicious. She'd been so hungry that macaroni and cheese probably would've been a feast.

Chance paid the bill, offered her a mint, and then helped her from her chair. His warm hand on her back and the spicy mint in her mouth had her remembering her promise to make out earlier. The thought made her shy and embarrassed. He probably dated cultured beauty queens who would never dream of saying something like that.

As they walked back to the hotel, Chance leaned down and murmured into her ear, "So, make out or hot tub?"

She giggled. "Or make out in the hot tub?"

He pumped his eyebrows. "Now you're talking."

She blushed as she remembered the bikini she'd found earlier. "Um, maybe not a great idea. Your assistant lady?"

"Yvonne."

"Yeah. The suit she got me does not cover up much."

"Even better."

She pushed at his arm. "You would say that. Can we please forget I asked you to go make out?"

"No." His eyes widened. "Why would we do that?"

Summer shook her head and stepped into the elevator. "Not one of my finest moments."

"I beg to differ."

She smiled at him. They reached their floor and Summer wouldn't mind kissing him again, not at all, but she felt like she'd ruined the mood with her make out comment. Made it all cheap and silly. "How about we go hot tub and we'll worry about the other part, um, later?" She stopped next to her door and pulled out her room key.

"Man." Chance placed a hand next to her head on the doorframe and leaned close. "You know how to elevate a guy's hopes, then dash them." His lips brushed her cheek. "All I could think about during dinner was kissing you."

Summer grasped the plastic room key tight, woozy from his lingering glance and his nearness. He smelled like the most intriguing mix of cedar, musk, and citrus. "Really?"

Chance simply nodded. Her body was trapped against the door, but she wasn't complaining. Chance cupped her face with his palms, trailing his thumbs along her cheeks. Summer dropped the room key, wrapped her hands around his back, and tugged him even closer. He grinned, then finished covering the distance and pressed his lips to hers. With his hands on her face, he gently tilted her head and quickly deepened the kiss. Summer stood on tiptoe and clung to him.

A door opened at the end of the hallway and pulled them apart. They were both breathing raggedly. A middle-aged couple sauntered by, giving them knowing glances.

Summer slipped out of his arms and bent down to retrieve her room key.

"Summer?" Chance whispered when she straightened.

She wasn't brave enough to look at him and see what power those eyes and that dimple had over her right now. "Yes," she muttered.

"Can I come in?"

"No." She glanced up in time to see the shock cross his face. "I'm not like that, Chance."

He nodded quickly. "I know. I just meant, well, I didn't mean—"

"What happened to the guy who said he was a good Christian boy and didn't want a piece of my tush?"

He smiled and trailed a hand down her face. "I didn't know how appealing your tush would be."

"Chance!" It was her turn to be shocked.

"I'm teasing. I really didn't mean come in, come in. More like can we please go to a place where we can kiss uninterrupted?" He winked, and she went hot and cold.

"Not a good idea."

"Okay." He nodded, though his lower lip protruded like a little boy denied candy. "Can we still go hot tub, or are you tired?"

Summer bit at her cheek and wanted to kiss that pouty lip. Chance was a good guy. One of the best, really. Too many times she'd been pushed to the limits of what intimacy she would allow before marriage. She didn't want to deal with defining boundaries and slowing this down with someone as appealing as Chance. She'd be in water hotter than any Jacuzzi. "Sure, let's hot tub."

"Perfect. See you in a few minutes." He walked across the hallway to his room.

Summer inserted the key card into the slot with trembling fingers. It would have been so easy to invite him in, but she'd traveled with boyfriends too often and her rule was always in effect: separate rooms and no kissing visitation rights. Hanging out in the hotel's main gathering areas was much, much safer, especially as tempting as Chance was to her.

She hurried through the living area and into the spacious bedroom, wrinkling her nose at the bikini she'd pulled out of one of the drawers earlier tonight. Flashing a lot of skin was not her usual mode of operation, but this dress had also shown flesh with a more daring neckline than she'd ever worn. She'd felt classy and pretty in the dress. She wasn't so sure about the suit.

Quickly changing, she eyed herself critically in the mirror. At least the bikini had good coverage of both ends. It was sporty with thick bands over the shoulder and under the chest, so it was really more her abdomen and lower back that were displayed instead of her cleavage and bare rear. She hated those suits that were so high in the back they were basically a thong.

She wrapped up in the hotel robe and slipped into the flip-flops she'd found in the closet. Chance's assistant was impressive. She'd need to send her a thank-you of some sort. When she'd asked if this was his usual, he hadn't said no. Her family had been pretty well off and her dad had been generous with her salary and royalties from toy sales, but she still wasn't used to staying in suites and having someone set up clothes, toiletries, and food for her.

A rap on her door announced Chance. She hurried through the suite and swung the door wide. Once again, her mouth was dry and her palms were sweating. He had on blue swim trunks and nothing else. His chest was very nice. Firm musculature and smooth skin.

"The assistant did better on your suit than mine," she managed to spit out.

Chance grabbed the tie of her robe and tugged her closer. "I'll be the judge of that."

"Don't!" she cried out, clinging to the robe to keep it closed.

"Come on, just a little sneak peek."

"No." Summer held her robe closed with one hand and pushed at his chest with the other. Yep, the skin felt as taut and smooth as it looked. My, oh my. Good thing he knew she wouldn't invite him in, or she'd be sorely tempted to break her rule. Just to kiss for a little while uninterrupted.

He laughed and reached for her hand. "You'll have to take the robe off sometime."

"I'm going to swim in it." She stuck her tongue out at him.

He led her down the hallway. "I'm sorry Yvonne didn't get you a suit you liked."

"Yvonne's amazing. I wasn't trying to complain, but the women you usually take on two-day dates and spoil rotten probably all wear bikinis."

Chance stopped before the elevator and faced her. "I've never taken a woman on a two-day date, or asked Yvonne to set something like this up before."

Summer's heart soared. Was he telling the truth? Was she something special to him? "You jerking with my heart?"

Chance chuckled. "I would never do that." He took a step closer. His strong body brushing against her.

Summer cinched the robe tighter. "How is Yvonne such an expert at this kind of thing, then? She had every little detail—makeup, hair products, perfume."

Chance's lips thinned. "My brother does this sort of thing all the time."

"Oh." She glanced at him from beneath her eyelashes. "But not you?"

He shook his head.

Summer flung her arms around his neck and kissed him soundly. "I like you, Chance Judd." She slipped out of his arms and pushed the elevator button.

Chance caught up to her quickly, and whirled her around. Pinning her against the wall, he took full advantage of her lips for several wonderful seconds. So many pleasure receptors were firing in her lips, she felt like she was floating with delight.

The elevator dinged open behind them. Summer thought they should just let it go to another floor. It would come back for them, eventually. A throat cleared, and the same middle-aged couple from earlier walked past them, both grinning broadly.

"Excuse us," Chance said, taking her hand again and leading her into the elevator.

Summer tried to catch her breath as the elevator whisked them down to the main level.

"We have got to find a spot where nobody can interrupt us," Chance muttered.

"I don't think that's such a good idea." Summer smiled at him.

Chance arched an eyebrow. "Depends on your version of a good idea."

Summer stepped closer, fully intent on kissing him again, when the elevator opened and some preteens rushed in. Chance led her out and down the hallway to the outdoor pool area. A few children were playing in the circular pool, but their parents were in the hot tub. Summer slipped her flip-flops off and dipped her toe in the pool. It was heated, but barely. She smiled at a little boy who climbed up onto the steps.

"Wanna watch me jump?" he asked.

"Sure."

He cannonballed off the steps and splashed her. She laughed. "Good one."

"You do it," the little guy said.

"Hudson," a beautiful young mom called from the hot tub. "Don't bother people."

"I'm not botherin' her, she's my friend!" He nodded to Summer. "Go."

Chance laughed next to her. "Your friend just called you out."

Summer gave him a death glare. She yanked her robe off, shoved it at Chance, and leapt into the pool, wrapping her arms around her legs and yelling, "Cannonball!" The cool water shocked her for a second, but she came up smiling.

Hudson cheered, "Good one!" He looked at Chance, who was watching her with a bemused expression. "Your turn."

"No." Chance shook his head. "It looks cold."

"You're gonna get shown up by a *girl?*"

Summer laughed as she beat her arms through the water to warm up. "Yeah, you loser."

Chance set her robe on a nearby lawn chair, ran to the edge of the pool, then smoothly dove in.

"No!" Hudson yelled out.

Summer tried to dodge, but Chance grabbed her in his arms as he surfaced. Being held by him with minimal clothing on was a bit too much fun. She tried to struggle free, but he held her and laughed. Water streamed down his handsome face, and she knew she was falling for him much too quickly.

"Lame!" Hudson said from the stairs. "Her splash was much better than yours."

"Says the five-year-old," Chance whispered roughly against her cheek. "This is the best move I've ever done."

"The twenty-six-year-old fully agrees." Summer cuddled against his chest.

"You gotta do something better than that," Hudson argued.

Chance gave her a mischievous grin, then tossed her into the air. Summer hit the water, flailing and sputtering.

"Yes," Hudson cheered. "Throw me!"

Summer wiped the water out of her eyes and watched the little boy launch himself into Chance's arms.

"Hudson," the mom warned.

"It's okay," Chance said. "If it's okay with you."

"Thanks." The mom blushed under Chance's smile. "But he can't swim very well."

"Can too," Hudson insisted.

"How about if I catch you?" Summer asked.

"Okay." He sighed heavily, then looked up at Chance. "Do it now!"

Chance tossed the cute little boy to Summer, and she spun him and flung him back. His peals of laughter almost made up for the fact that Summer had been launched out of Chance's arms because of him. A little while later, Hudson's mom told him it was time to go. He climbed out of the pool, protesting. She made him thank both of them. Both mother and son gave Chance longing glances as they left.

Summer splashed him. "I think you made some fans."

Chance brushed a hand through his short hair. "Five-year-olds are pretty easy to please."

"I was talking about the mom."

Chance winked. "Jealous?"

"Maybe."

He swam toward her, but she dodged and pulled herself out of the pool. The hot tub still had a few adults in it, but the pool was empty now.

Summer wrapped her arms around her torso, not comfortable in the sporty bikini.

Chance climbed out next to her. "Cold?"

"I told you I don't usually wear bikinis."

Chance arched his eyebrows. "Everyone else's loss."

She rolled her eyes at him, but felt warm inside. They climbed the concrete steps to where the hot tub overlooked the pool and said hello to the three occupants who greeted them, but left a few minutes later.

"Ah, this is what I'm talking about," Summer murmured, the hot water embracing her tired body.

"It is nice," Chance said, closing his eyes and sinking down deeper.

"Nice? This whole day has been unreal. Thank you."

Chance smiled at her and took her hand, holding it under the water. "Thanks for letting me kidnap you."

"Anytime." And she found she meant it. This break from reality had been exactly what she needed, but being with Chance was the best part. "Must be nice being a millionaire and able to do amazing things like this." She gestured to the beautiful hotel, though she meant the entire day.

He didn't respond, just gave her a smile that showed she was way off.

"Oh no." She gulped and released his hand. "You're a billionaire."

Chance shrugged.

Summer took a long breath. A billionaire? She closed her eyes and let the jets pound at her back as it all came rushing back. That stupid billionaire bride pact. Curse Erin for ever thinking of it. The thing had haunted almost all of her friends now. Her eyes popped open and she glanced at the handsome man next to her, who luckily had his eyes closed. Was she going to be next? The water was suddenly too hot, but she didn't want to sit on the side and show off her abdomen, so she stayed in her spot, squeezing her eyes shut again and sweating it out.

Okay, so maybe her girl's camp friends would say the pact haunted them in good ways. Most of them were happily married to wealthy men and doing great things with their lives. Erin, MacKenzie, and Taylor were the only ones so far who hadn't married money, but they were also ecstatically happy. Yet Summer was not ready to follow the trend. She was a trendsetter, not a follower. She wanted to be successful all on her own, and would've been if it hadn't been for that cursed Mumford's Sons company talking her dad into selling to the shark, Lillywhite, who proceeded to fire her.

She finally opened her eyes to Chance staring at her. "You okay?" he asked.

She nodded quickly, but the magical spell of the day was broken. Chance was a great guy, if Summer was looking to be some rich guy's arm candy. She could enjoy being with him, but she needed to be more in control when he kissed her and held her. Maybe someday she'd have a chance with the seemingly perfect Chance. Right now, she needed to focus on finding her own way.

CHAPTER EIGHT

THE DAY AFTER BIKING, THEY'D TAKEN A QUICK PLANE RIDE BACK TO Gunnison, and Yvonne had made sure Chance's rented Land Rover, with the bikes loaded on the rack, was waiting for him at the airport so they could get back to Crested Butte. She was really good at this sort of thing. Chance had found an online site that did flowers, chocolates, and gifts, and sent her a huge basket to thank her. He also made sure he was caught up on any work Yvonne had for him before he left his house to come find Summer.

He'd had the best day with Summer yesterday. After the hot tub, she was exhausted, so they'd each gone to their own rooms to shower and go to bed. He had been feeling the long day too, and he tried not to second-guess her slight change in demeanor. Before she'd pled tired, things had been rolling so quickly he was sure he would get the kiss of a lifetime to finish off the day. As it was, he'd given her a quick kiss before she'd slipped into her room. A disappointment to be sure, but hopefully not a worry.

While Chance was daydreaming about how she'd looked in the swimming suit last night, Summer ran out of her front door at the ranch and jumped into his rented Land Rover. "Hey, wait," he said. "I'm supposed to get your door."

"Trevor is ticked at me for staying overnight with you and not making it to church. You better drive now or you'll have a shotgun in your face."

"Seriously?"

"Drive!" She thumped her palms on the dash.

Chance jumped. He dropped it into gear and pulled quickly out of the driveway. "I should go talk to him if he's upset."

"Oh, no way." Summer shook her head. "Not if you know what's good for you. He takes overprotective to a level any dad of a teenage girl would be proud of."

Chance glanced at her and saw the twinkle in those blue eyes. "You just love to tease me."

"Go back to that ranch and see if I'm teasing you or not."

"Maybe when I drop you off Trevor and I can have a heart-to-heart."

"Brave, brave man." She winked. "Your legs sore?"

"A little bit." Chance was glad she was back to teasing and being her fun self. He'd been a little worried last night after the hot tub and his revelation that he was a billionaire. Most women would be excited about that prospect, but it obviously bothered Summer. "You're really making me hike? I thought we both agreed mountain biking is much more fun."

"True, but I'm saddle sore. Never take a two-month siesta from biking, then go for seven hours."

Chance's face reddened. She would say just about anything. "Which way?"

"Let's go to Judd River Falls. The hike named after you." She winked. "It's a short, perfect Sunday hike, and we can continue up the trail toward Copper Creek Lake if you're up to it. Drive to the same place you parked yesterday."

"Gotcha." They drove up the road, and he enjoyed the casual camaraderie they had. Summer liked to tease him, but she was allowing him to date her, to be part of her life, and to kiss her. He'd take a little teasing for all of that.

He parked the vehicle and they ambled slowly up the incline to the falls, pausing to look down at the rushing water for a while, then continued up the trail.

"See?" she said after they'd been quiet and enjoyed the scenery of quaking aspen, pine trees, and the majestic mountains. "This is a good way to ease your legs out of that stiffness."

"And it's beautiful scenery."

"Yep. I chose well."

They were alone on the trail, nothing but green surrounding them and the river rushing by down below. "And it's private." He stopped, grabbed her around the waist, and pulled her in.

Summer gave a little gasp of surprise, but her happy smile appeared quickly. "Just try and kiss me. I bet within twenty seconds somebody comes around one of those bends to interrupt us. It's our curse."

"Dang for curses," he whispered against her mouth. "I'd better not waste time if I've only got twenty seconds." He claimed her lips with his, and she didn't disappoint as she snuggled into his arms and matched him kiss for kiss.

A little while later, crashing and yelling came from above them. They broke apart. Summer pursed her lips. "That was a good one. We got a hundred and thirty-two seconds before the interruption."

"If you were counting the entire time, I am doing something wrong."

Summer laughed, taking his hand and swinging their arms like a child as they said hello to the young family trooping down the trail.

As soon as they passed, Chance tugged her closer. "Summer. Please say you weren't counting."

Summer tilted her head to the side and grinned at him. Long seconds ticked by before she wrapped her arms around his neck and murmured in his ear, "I wasn't counting."

"So I wasn't doing something wrong?" He encompassed her back with his hands. She fit perfectly in his arms.

"On the contrary, my unconfident friend. You were doing everything just right."

Chance smiled and decided to try it again, just to make sure.

Summer loved this relaxed Sunday afternoon with Chance. They only went up the trail a couple of miles before heading back, holding hands and talking the entire time. The scenery was gorgeous with cascading pines on the mountainside and the creek trickling below them on the other side of the trail. She'd pushed future worries to the back of her mind, intent on enjoying this time with Chance. It bugged her that he was a billionaire and she was a destitute loser with no future prospects for work, but it wasn't his fault.

"If I ask you to come back to my place for dinner, will you give me a hard time?" Chance asked when they reached his Land Rover.

"I'll always give you a hard time, but you can ask." She leaned against the vehicle.

Chance bent down and kissed her. She returned it wholeheartedly for several minutes before giving him a playful grin, slipping out of his arms and into the car. Chance shut the door and hurried around to his side. He didn't start the car, but focused on her. "Summer. I'd love to cook you dinner, and I promise not to try anything inappropriate. Will you please come to my place?"

"Smooth, Judd. Real smooth."

"And?"

She bit at her cheek to hide a smile. "I'll think about it."

"Think about it? We've only got a ten-minute drive before we'll be back at your house."

"Ooh, good point. I don't want to face Papa Turnbow yet. Let's go to your rented mansion, then. I know how you love to boast about all your money." She winked to show she was teasing. He actually didn't flaunt his money, and she liked that. "Be warned, though: if you try anything inappropriate, you'd better be prepared to lose an eyeball or something."

Chance chuckled. "Noted."

He drove them down the mountain, taking her hand and resting it on his muscled thigh. Summer found her thoughts scattered by the simple move. He could do that to her so effectively with the slightest touch. She'd better be on her guard at his house.

He drove northeast of downtown up into the gated community for the ultra-rich. When he pulled through the circular drive and into the garage of a massive house with a pond to the side, grass stretching all around, and an unreal view of the ski resort, she tried for nonchalant. "Too much, Judd. Maybe you shouldn't have brought me to the mansion. It is intimidating."

Chance shook his head. "You can handle it. I've seen you deal with a lot worse than this."

Summer wasn't sure she could deal with it. He got her door, took her hand, and led her through the spotless five-car garage with only the Land Rover, his two bikes, and a utility vehicle of some sort to fill the space. They walked through a large mud room with an impressive laundry room and bathroom attached. All the cabinets were white and the walls were painted a pale blue. It had a great vacation feel. Then they entered the great room, and her jaw dropped. It was massive, with three-story windows showcasing the mountains, knotty cherry cabinets and woodwork throughout. The plush leather sofas looked comforting. The walls were painted a neutral grayish-brown, with landscape paintings providing bursts of color here and there. There was a rock and granite fireplace that ran the height of the three stories. She loved the entire thing.

She forced a confidence she wasn't feeling, strode to a sofa, and plopped down. "I'll just hang here while you cook for me."

Chance smiled. "Would you like the remote to the TV or the fireplace?"

"No, the view's enough of a show for me."

"It is pretty. You could always go sit in the hot tub."

"I don't like the suits you give me to wear in the hot tub."

He laughed. "I liked the one for last night enough for the both of us."

Summer chose to ignore that. Chance started pulling things out of the industrial fridge. He piled the containers in his arms and walked to some patio doors. Summer couldn't just sit there. She rushed to him as he struggled to open the door with his arms full and swung it wide.

"Thank you." He set the packages down on the counter next to a built-in grill.

Summer glanced around the patio and was awestruck again. "The cabinets out here are nicer than my parents' house."

Chance pushed a button to light the grill, not answering her. How did she expect him to respond? Her parents had plenty of money and a beautiful home, but this place was amazing. If Chance was really a billionaire, his home or homes were probably nicer than this.

She glanced over at the pile on the counter as he started unwrapping the packages—steak, seasoned chicken, huge shrimp, veggies ready to grill. "Wow. You know how to grill, eh?"

"Easy when it's all pre-packaged. I didn't know what you liked, so I bought a little of everything."

"So you just assumed I'd say yes and come to dinner tonight?"

"I hoped."

"And what are you going to do with all the leftovers?"

"I can eat them for dinner tomorrow."

"Liar. You'll be waiting for me outside of Sugar 'n' Spice tomorrow, ready to take me out somewhere."

Chance laughed. "You've got me all figured out."

Summer rested her hands on his chest. "For the most part. Too much brains, too much money, too much looks, too much brawn."

Chance's dimple deepened. "Your grammar is atrocious, sweetheart, but I sure do appreciate the compliments."

Summer blushed at the endearment. She gave him a quick peck on the lips and dropped her hands.

Chance reached for her, tugging her back in. "Hopefully you'll never say too much kissing."

"I don't think that's possible."

Chance pressed his lips to hers, and she didn't think anything about him was too much. The grill was burning hot by the time they pulled apart. Chance loaded the grill up with meat and vegetables while Summer watched him.

"So, are your other houses as beautiful as this rental?" she asked.

Chance nodded. "Byron thought I was crazy to come here when I could've gone and stayed in one of my other homes, but I wanted something different, something ... amazing." He studied her.

"Did you find it?" She could hardly catch a breath when he looked at her like that.

"I think so."

"It is plural, then?" Summer needed to change the subject. Had he really found something amazing with her? Had either of them been looking for this? It was all too new and exciting to dissect and think about too much. Maybe talking or thinking about it would ruin the magic.

"Plural?" he asked.

"You have houses?"

"Oh. Yes, I do." He didn't say it like he was bragging, just a fact of life.

"Where are these houses?"

"Charlotte, Kauai, and Jackson Hole."

"Yet you've never been to Costa Rica?"

"Nope."

"I guess there are some things I can still show you."

"There are a lot of things you can show me." He arched an eyebrow at her and started her direction.

Summer backed slowly away. "You've got meat hands. No touchy-touch."

Chance ran at her, holding his hands up like Frankenstein. "Bloody meat hands want to touchy-touch the pretty lady."

Summer shrieked and ran across the patio and to the grass. She was almost around the side of the house and to the pond when Chance caught her, lifting her off the ground and spinning her around. "Meat hands, so gross," Summer panted out.

"I didn't know you were a germaphobe."

"Just about raw meat."

Chance didn't release her. "Give me a kiss and I'll let you go sanitize where I touched." His hands were around her waist.

"Only if you promise to sanitize your hands too."

"I promise."

She kissed him good and long before squirming away. "Okay, now go wash."

"Anything else I can do for another kiss?"

"You're pretty willing to promise your life away."

"For a kiss from you?" He grinned and his dimple was on fine display. "Definitely."

Her phone beeped in her pocket.

"Check it while I go wash my hands." He winked.

Summer pulled it from her pocket, wandering idly back toward the patio as she read the message from one of her recent boyfriends, Jerome.

I know you said you needed a break, but I think it's been long enough. I miss you, beautiful lady. We've got a great group backpacking through Europe in August. I think Taylor and Lane are going to commit. Say you're in. I'll massage your sore muscles every night if you'll let me.

Summer rolled her eyes and pocketed her phone. Her lips drew into a thin line. Jerome. He was a lot of fun to be with, but he took nothing serious. She'd been finished with him weeks before she'd finally admitted she needed a break.

Chance exited the house and smiled at her. Summer wondered if she'd ever tire of him like she had all the others. "Everything okay?" he asked.

"Yeah, just an old ... friend asking me to come tour Europe." She gave him a wan smile.

"Friend?" Chance turned his back on her, lifted the lid on the grill, and started flipping meat and stirring the veggies on the metal tray. He glanced over at her.

Summer squirmed, then blew out her breath. "I dated him for a while."

"Are you going?" Chance bit out.

"Of course I'm not going. Are you daft?"

His back stiffened, but he didn't respond.

"I miss traveling and would love to go, but I've got to find a design job where I can work remotely so I can see the world again." Traveling was spendy and flexible jobs like she'd had weren't easy to come by.

Chance closed the grill and slowly turned. His usually warm eyes were chilly like the Arctic Sea. "If money wasn't an option, you'd be off on your adventures with a different boyfriend every week?"

Summer blinked at him, not sure how to respond. The answer was probably an affirmative, but maybe she didn't want a different boyfriend each week, if she could be with Chance.

"How many have there been?" Chance muttered.

"Adventures?" Summer asked, certain that wasn't what he was asking.

Chance shook his head.

"What do you want me to say?" Summer folded her arms across her chest. "I've lived my life, Chance, and yes, I've dated a lot of different men. Like you haven't dated anyone? Like you've just been waiting your entire life for me."

Chance shrugged. "You're right. I've dated. I just ..." He glanced down at the concrete. "You're special to me, Summer, and I can just imagine how many men have chased you throughout your life. It's hard not to allow myself to be jealous."

Summer walked across the patio and cupped his chin with her palm. He glanced up at her. "Not to inflate your hopes, big boy, but you're pretty special to me too."

Chance placed his hand over hers and kissed her gently. The meat sizzled behind them, and it was only when a distinctive burning odor rose up that they finally pulled apart, laughing and not certain if their relationship had gone to a better level or not.

CHAPTER NINE

CHANCE GRINNED AS HE WALKED DOWN CRESTED BUTTE'S MAIN street Monday afternoon, though his legs were a bit stiff from the bike ride Saturday and the hike Sunday.

He arrived at Sugar 'n' Spice, walked in the open door, and glanced around. The shop was empty. It was a nice store, it just didn't fit Summer. She was a free spirit who needed to design and wander. That made him worry about them almost as much as the uncertainty of being compared to a bunch of different men. Was she a female version of Byron? Now that was uncalled for. He couldn't compare his fun, beautiful Summer to his brother.

Adding all the worries together, including his involvement in her family business demise, did the two of them stand a chance? Besides coming on this trip to escape, he was grounded and practical. He traveled a little bit, usually to one of his own houses, but for the most part he stayed close to home and worked hard. He didn't want to capture Summer and pin her down, but he didn't know how he'd fit in her life as a wanderer.

He shook his head. He'd only known her a few weeks. He was the one acting like Byron, thinking he'd found his soul mate after a couple great experiences with a woman. Summer really was something special, though, the most fabulous woman he'd ever met.

The back door of the shop, which led into a storage area, swung open. A man who dwarfed Summer both in height and muscles held the door and a large box. Summer's arms were laden with boxes. The top box started to slip.

"Help," Summer cried out.

Chance started forward, but the guy grabbed the box before Chance could reach them.

Summer looked up at the burly guy and laughed. Jealousy ripped through Chance's gut, and he froze mid-step. Who was this guy and why was he helping Summer? He knew she'd burned through men before him. Was she already moving on from Chance?

The two of them set the boxes by the desk and finally noticed Chance.

"Hi," Summer offered. Was it his imagination, or did she look guilty?

The big guy gave him a friendly smile. Jerk.

"Who is this guy?" Chance bit out.

Summer's mouth dropped open. Then her eyes narrowed. "Wow, really? You're going to accuse me like that with no knowledge of the situation?"

The man smirked at Summer and folded his muscular arms across his chest. That's when Chance noticed the wide white-gold band on his left ring finger. The guy was married? What in the world was Summer doing?

"Do you need any more help, sweetheart?" the man asked.

Summer shook her head and rolled her eyes. "No. Thanks for *everything*."

"See you later, darlin'."

Chance glared at the large man as he brushed past him, still grinning like this was all some big joke. He turned the force of that glare on Summer. True, they weren't committed for life after three weeks, but he couldn't believe the Summer he thought he knew would date a married man, and he felt nauseated at the thought of her dating anyone but him.

"Don't look at me like that. I haven't done anything wrong." She bent down and ripped the packing tape off the box.

"Are you ..." He swallowed, not wanting to verbalize it and tick her off, but she'd dated a lot of men. Maybe this was normal for her. "Dating a married man?" His stomach churned. All those feelings she'd given him—joy, passion, excitement. She was worse than Byron; his brother would never date a married woman. Chance needed to walk away now before he exploded.

"Oh, heavens," Summer grunted out. She stood and faced him. "I've told you about Isaac. He's married to one of my best friends, MacKenzie."

"And that makes it better!" Chance shoved a hand through his hair and turned away, pacing in front of her. "I thought you were different. This amazing free spirit, beautiful, funny, and genuine. But you're ..." He couldn't even spit it out, that would make it true.

"Chance!" Summer grasped his arm and pulled him to a stop. "Listen to the words coming out of my mouth, you imbecile! Isaac is married to one of my best friends, and even if he wasn't, I would never date a married man. Isaac is a huge tease, and I'm sure when he saw you all defensive and the first words out of your mouth are, 'Who is this guy?' he saw a chance to give me a hard time."

The breath rushed out of him and all Chance could do was stare at her. "Are you serious?" he finally muttered.

"Yes. He and MacKenzie are very happily married and he's like a big brother to me."

"I'm ... sorry?" Oh, he was sorry, but he was also so relieved he could hardly stay upright.

"You should be. First of all, you insult me and think I would date a married guy. Second of all, you compliment me and say I'm amazing, beautiful, funny, and genuine. What am I supposed to do with all of that?"

"Go to dinner with me tonight?" Chance had to try to salvage this. He'd offended her, understandably. He didn't usually have insecurities, but he wanted Summer all to himself—forever, if he were being honest. Letting himself dwell on her past had pushed him in the wrong direction. "Somewhere nice. Where I actually come and pick you up instead of just waiting outside the store and hoping you'll say yes."

Summer harrumphed. "Oh, yeah?" Her eyebrows tilted in a challenge and she took a step toward him. "And if I say no?"

"You'll break my heart." He reached for her hand and she gave it to him.

"Oh, that was cheesy, Judd." She squeezed his hand and smiled. "You come by the house about seven and I'll see if I can fit you in."

"I'll be there." The anxiety over her dating some married guy disappeared, followed closely by anticipation to spend more time with her tonight. He knew a woman had never reeled him in this quickly before. He prayed she'd never let him go.

He left the shop, walked quickly back to the Land Rover, and drove to his rental house. After working for the next few hours on Byron's requests, he finally forced himself to call his brother.

"Hey. How's the chickie?" Byron greeted him with.

The name grated on Chance, but he didn't take the bait. "She's an amazing lady."

"So you took my advice and lied?"

That hit him harder. He had taken Byron's advice. "No, not really. I just ... haven't told her everything yet."

Byron chortled. "You lied. I'm proud of you, bro. Going against the Judd moral code to get a woman."

Chance's stomach churned. He changed the subject quick. "Hey, I need your help. Remember that toy company you worked with a few years ago, where you dated the CEO?"

"Yeah, Marissa Yates is the CEO. KJ's Fun Zone."

"Do you have any contacts there that don't hate you?"

"Like I'm so hateable."

"You know I didn't mean that. Everyone loves you, but I know you dated Marissa so she's probably still mooning over you."

"I wish." Byron gave a loud sigh.

Chance was surprised at the longing in his brother's voice. There was a story with Marissa, and he'd really like to hear it after he helped Summer out.

"Marissa and I have kept in contact. We're friends," Byron admitted. "She's a … great person."

"Wow. The maturity of that astounds me."

"Thank you." Chance could almost picture his brother bowing and smirking at him.

"Can you send me her contact info?"

"You're trying to help out your new girl?"

"It's the right thing to do." Chance couldn't wait to see her face if this all worked out.

"If you say so. But coming from someone with a lot more experience—ahem, me—women don't generally like it when you try to take control of their lives. Just love on them and let them live, I say."

Chance cringed. His brother's theories were not his. Okay, so he had sort of taken Byron's advice and not told Summer the entire truth, or any version of the truth. He would rectify that soon, but first he needed to set things up to find her a great job. If she decided to travel the world after she had the job, maybe he'd have to follow her.

CHAPTER TEN

SUMMER UNPACKED DECORATIVE YARD SIGNS AND DAYDREAMED about dinner tonight with Chance. Was she crazy to want to pursue this relationship? She'd be insane not to. He was a fabulous guy who treated her right, made her laugh, kissed like a champion, and was handsome and successful to boot. Most people would say she was crazy not to run into his arms, yet she still wanted to be successful on her own. She laughed at herself. As if Chance was proposing or something.

Her cell phone rang. She pulled it out and studied the unfamiliar number. She didn't usually get telemarketers. "Hello," she said tersely.

"Miss Anderson?"

"Yes." Should she just hang up or let the person get their spiel out? They probably didn't want to be working as a telemarketer so she always tried to be nice.

"This is Marissa Yates with KJ's Fun Zone."

Summer about dropped the phone. She knew exactly who Marissa Yates was: CEO of her father's biggest competition. Summer had a lot of respect for the company and the woman running it. She'd debated emailing them her résumé, but they were a lot larger than the companies she'd approached so far and she'd had little luck with the other companies. Everyone either said they couldn't afford her, they didn't design their own toys, or they already had a designer on staff.

"Um, yes?" She had no clue how to respond.

"It's my understanding that Magical Dream Toys did not keep you on as a designer after the buyout."

"No, they did not." Was she just calling to rub it in? Sheesh.

"Have you already committed to another toy company?"

"No." Summer paced the shop, not sure where this conversation was going, but her hopes were rising by the second.

"Would you be interested in working with me?"

"Yes," Summer squeaked out, her throat dry and her heart pumping.

"I'm glad to hear that." Marissa gave a warm laugh. "You probably know that we're located in Hudson, Ohio. I don't expect you to relocate; I understand you can design from anywhere, and we can make that work."

"Thanks," Summer breathed out. Holy cow, this really was a dream come true.

"Could you fly in next week and fill out the paperwork, share your designs with us, and get to know my team? From there we can figure out how often we'd need you to come in and set up a schedule with production."

"Sure." Summer glanced around the home décor store almost in shock. She'd just been offered the perfect job.

"Where are you located currently?"

"Crested Butte, Colorado."

"Can you text your email and location to me at this number and we'll set up the flights and hotels? Would Monday through Wednesday of next week work with your schedule?"

"Yes." Summer realized she'd given pretty much one-word answers throughout this conversation. Luckily Marissa didn't seem put off by it. Toy designers could be a socially reclusive lot, but Summer was excited to meet this woman in person and show her she did have some conversational skills. "Thank you for this opportunity," she said.

"We're excited," Marissa said. "It's perfect timing for us, as one of our designers is out on maternity leave and just informed me she might not be coming back. And if she does, it'll only be a fraction of what she produced before."

Summer didn't know how she'd gotten so lucky, but she wasn't going to complain.

Chance pulled into the ranch yard and killed the engine. He hoped the good news Summer had gotten earlier today would have her throwing herself into his arms. A guy could dream.

He swung open the car door and stared into the wrong end of a shotgun.

"Step out nice and easy there, cowboy."

The older guy backed up a step and Chance followed his instructions. His hands lifted automatically into the air, and he would've laughed at the cliché, but it felt like the right thing to do when an obviously unstable man was pointing a gun in his face.

"Now tell me real simple like what you're doing on my property."

"I'm, um ..." Chance cleared his throat. "Picking up Summer for dinner."

"Ah, I thought so." The guy sized him up, still staring down the barrel. "You're the yahoo who kept her overnight, made her miss church, and is making her smile all the time."

Chance would've smiled if he didn't have a shotgun pointed at his face. "I apologize for making her miss church, but we stayed in our own rooms, sir. I promise I did nothing inappropriate."

The man studied him for a few uncomfortable seconds, then lowered the gun and extended his hand. "Trevor Turnbow."

"Chance Judd." Chance shook his hand, relief washing over him. It looked like he wasn't getting shot.

"See you don't make her smile *too* much. You catch my drift, boy?"

"Yes, sir."

"Lay off him, Papa Turnbow," Summer called from the porch. "The whole shotgun thing is only funny when they're losers."

"It's always funny," Trevor muttered.

Chance hadn't even heard the door open. He turned, and was overcome with the beauty of this woman. She'd looked unreal in the dress and bikini Yvonne had picked out for her Saturday night, but Summer's natural look fit her even better. Her dress looked soft and flowed from her chest down to her knees, showing off her fit, tanned legs. The dark gray set off her blonde hair and deep blue eyes. "You're so beautiful," he managed to say.

"I bet you say that to all the girls." She descended the steps, clutching a red purse and grinning shyly at him.

"No, I really don't. You're something special, Summer."

Trevor harrumphed beside him. "I know you're not going to keep your hands off, but you keep them in respectable places. Got it, son?"

Chance forced himself to be respectful, drag his eyes from Summer, and look at the man as he responded. "Yes, sir."

Summer whacked Trevor with her small purse. "I can take care of myself, old man."

"And I'll protect my girls no matter what they say," Trevor shot back at her.

Summer just laughed at him and walked toward Chance's Land Rover. "I know you will, Papa Turnbow, and it's one of the many reasons I love you so much."

"Love you too," Trevor grunted out before nodding to Chance and sauntering toward the larger house.

Chance hurried to get Summer's door. She stopped and faced him before getting in.

"You look all ... lit up," Chance said, wanting to check if Trevor was far enough away that he could steal a kiss.

"Oh, Chance, I have the best news!" She threw her arms around his neck. "I got offered my perfect job today."

Chance hoped his face didn't reveal his involvement. He grinned at her. "Congrats!"

"I'm beyond ecstatic. It's the company that rivaled my dad's and I love the toys they put out. The CEO is this way cool lady and I cannot wait to work with her."

Chance squeezed her closer. "You deserve it. I can't wait to see what you create."

"Thanks. I've got a bunch of designs done that I can share with them on Monday. Marissa is flying me to Ohio to sign paperwork and meet with her teams. I'm not even sure if their production team is on site or in China, but honestly, I don't even care, I'm so excited to be working in my field again."

Chance smiled at her, but felt a little pang. "You're leaving in a week?"

"You gonna miss me?"

"You have no idea." He lowered his head and claimed her lips. Several minutes later, he'd explored her mouth with his own and decided he loved the soft material of this dress as his hands moved over her back.

"Hands in respectable places," Trevor barked from behind them.

Summer jumped from his arms. "Trevor! Honestly, you're not actually my dad, you know?"

"Tell that to somebody who cares." He glared at Chance. "If you're gonna make out with her in my driveway, what are you going to do when you get her alone? Do I need to cock this thing again?" The shotgun was still in his hands.

"No, sir. I promise I will keep myself under control." Chance fought a smile, finding himself liking this gruff old guy. He definitely had Summer's best interest in mind, and so did Chance.

"See that you do, because if you don't ..." He hefted the gun. "I really like to use him."

"Oh my, enough with the threats. Goodbye, Papa Turnbow."

"No 'love you'?" Trevor asked with an undeniable smirk.

"Not right now, you old coot." Summer slid into the sport utility.

Chance shut her door and turned to Trevor. "Thank you, sir, for watching out for her."

Trevor nodded. "See that you treat her with respect."

"I plan on it."

Trevor gestured him away. Chance strode around the car, smiling. Summer had her dream job and he was going to spend the night with her. He'd treat with her respect, but he was definitely getting his share of kissing in tonight as well.

CHAPTER ELEVEN

SUMMER TOOK A BITE OF A GOOEY MOZZARELLA STICK AT Marchitelli's Gourmet Noodle. The marinara sauce blended perfectly with the warm cheese. She glanced around the restaurant with white tablecloths, wood flooring, and black cloth draping the ceiling and walls. She loved that Crested Butte was so laid-back that this yummy Italian restaurant was upscale.

She and Chance were snuggled into a booth, the black leather smooth against her bare legs. It was intimate and perfect. She took a sip of her water and focused on the handsome face she'd grown so accustomed to the past few weeks. "I feel like I've known you forever, but we really don't know each other that well."

Chance nodded. "I feel the same, but I definitely want to get to know you better." He winked, and Summer all but melted into the seat.

"Sometimes when I'm with you I feel like I'm in a Nicholas Sparks movie."

He arched an eyebrow. "Channing Tatum again?"

"Yeah, but you're much better-looking than him."

"Thanks." He chuckled.

He glanced around as if checking if someone was watching, then pulled her in close and kissed her gently. Summer wrapped her arms around his neck and tugged him in. Chance was definitely the complete package for her. She didn't mind if he was a suit, if he could kiss like this.

They pulled apart when the waitress came and took their orders, giving each other conspiratorial smiles.

Summer excused herself to use the restroom. She was washing her hands when her phone beeped in her purse. Pulling it out, she stared at the text from Marissa. She'd sent a text a few hours ago asking how her new boss found out she wasn't working with Magical Dream Toys anymore.

The reply wasn't what she expected.

My friend, Byron Judd of Mumford's Sons, said his brother had told him all about you and asked that he recommend you to me.

Byron ... Judd? Mumford's Sons? It couldn't be any relation to Chance. No, it really couldn't. That would be too horrible. Yet who was this brother who'd recommended her? She tapped out a quick response.

Do you mind me asking how you know Byron and who his brother is? I only know Mumford's Sons through my father.

It might've been a gutsy thing to ask her new boss, but she needed to get to the bottom of this. She really wished she knew nothing about Mumford's Sons. The slimeballs, anyway. Her phone beeped.

I dated Byron for a very short time, and then we became friends. His brother is Chance Judd. From everything Byron says, Chance is a great guy.

Summer stared at the phone in shock for several seconds. Finally she managed to tap out, *Thanks.*

Her hands trembled as she punched in the single-word response. She stowed the phone in her purse, not waiting for Marissa's reply. Glancing in the mirror, she didn't like the way her cheeks were spotted with color and her eyes were full of rage. Just the mention of Mumford's Sons riled her up.

She splashed a little water on her cheeks and ran her hands under cold water, but it didn't help much. Chance. It couldn't be true. Her Chance was related to this Byron, part of the Mumford's Sons who ruined her life. Her dad had dealt with the company who sold them out; Summer had been traveling in Europe at the time. She didn't have any input until it was over and her job and lifestyle were gone. If Chance was really one of Mumford's Sons ... A strangled yelp rose from her throat. "Aargh!"

A lady entered the bathroom and eyed her strangely. Summer couldn't find the strength to apologize or even smile.

She took a deep breath, then rushed from the restroom. As she approached their table, Chance looked up with a warm smile. His dimple was on fine display, but instead of wanting to touch it like usual, she wanted to jab her finger into it and scream at him.

"What's your brother's name?" she rushed out, not sitting down.

Chance stared at her warily, gripping his napkin in his fingers. "Byron."

Summer didn't move for half a second, rage filling her chest. It was true. Her perfect man was a liar and a skunk. No! How could life be so unfair?

She closed her eyes and took a steadying breath, finally opening them and muttering, "You've known this whole time who I was?"

Chance's eyes were wary. He stood slowly. He cut a fine figure in a blue button-down shirt untucked over dark pants with his handsome face and those blue-green eyes she used to want to get lost in. It just went to show that you should never trust anyone, especially if they looked as good as he did to her. Tears of frustration sprang to her eyes and she dashed them away. Dang him.

"Summer." He held his hands up. "I only knew Mr. Anderson's daughter as Gabriella. When I figured it out, I was already falling for you. I promise I was going to tell you, but I wanted to give *us* a chance before you found out and there was no chance of developing a relationship."

Summer shook her head at him. Gabriella. She hated that name and only used it for legal documents. His excuse was lame and full of nothing but a shallow guy wanting to have his way with a dumb girl. She refused to be the dumb girl.

"Well." She took a long breath, pinning him with her eyes. "There's definitely no *chance* now. I could never be with someone who would blatantly lie to me." She grabbed her glass of water and flung it in his face.

He blinked away the moisture but didn't move. "Summer, please."

"Don't you please me!" she screamed. "Aagh! I *hate* Mumford's Sons!"

"Summer. Let me explain." He reached out a hand.

She jerked away from his touch like it was a hot iron. "No! There will be no explaining. You lied to me!"

Pivoting from his beseeching glance, she ran out of the restaurant and into the night. If she ever saw Chance Judd of Mumford's Sons again, she'd give him a lot more than a glass of water in the face.

CHAPTER TWELVE

CHANCE WATCHED THE DOOR BANG CLOSED BEHIND SUMMER. Water dripped down his neck and into his collar. He laid a hundred-dollar bill on the table and walked out, ignoring the sideways glances directed at him. Shuffling out into the night, he spotted her fleeing down Main Street. His heart twisted.

What had he expected? He knew this revelation would rip Summer away from him, and it had. He could blame Byron for telling him to lie, but Chance was the one who listened. The one who didn't stand up for what was right. He hung his head and walked slowly down the street, wishing he could chase after her but knowing it would do no good. Maybe Trevor would come after him with a shotgun again. He wouldn't blame the old man at all.

The next few days were miserable. He wanted to go to her, but thought better of it. Would time help her to forgive him? To remember the good times they had and at least listen to his side? He didn't know if his side was any better. It was his and his brother's fault that her dad had sold the company and caused the ensuing fallout with Lillywhite, but her dad had come to them, knowing they were the best. He'd wanted to sell and they'd helped him get top dollar. Just because they'd made a substantial fee on the transaction wasn't Chance's fault. It was how the business worked and what her father had agreed to, and honestly he'd been more than happy with it.

Friday night he couldn't take it any longer. He drove to her little house and pounded on the door. Summer flung it open, dressed in a T-shirt and yoga pants, her golden hair swept up in a ponytail. She looked unbelievably good.

Her eyes swept up and down him before resting on his face with a belligerent expression. She folded her arms across her chest. "What? Did you come here to tell me you went by my family home and stabbed our dog, Betsy? That's about the only thing worse you could do to me."

Chance blinked and slowly shook his head. "I never wanted to hurt you, Summer."

"Yes, you did. Before you knew me, you couldn't have cared less about ripping my life apart."

"Your father came to us. We helped him improve the company's image and profitability and he sold for four times what he could've on his own. The people who bought Magical Dream Toys promised they would keep you and your brother on staff. I didn't know they only wanted your designs and weren't willing to pay you what you were worth."

She straightened, and standing a step above him in the doorframe, she was almost as tall as him. "You're some almighty lawyer. Why didn't you insist on written contracts?"

He hung his head. "You're right. I should have. Your father and the new owner both claimed we'd keep 'business as usual.' It was only after everything was signed and done that the new owner revealed what a snake he was and started dismantling your father's work. I'm sorry he basically stole all your designs."

"You're right in league with him. How much did you and your brother make off of Magical Dream Toys?"

Chance swallowed and looked away. He didn't need to tell her, but he found himself muttering, "Five million." He didn't tell her that's only what he had personally walked away with, not including what Byron and their company had cleared.

"Pocket change to you."

He didn't answer. She was kind of right. It was a smaller deal, but it had never set right with him. He'd wanted to go after the new owner and get Summer and her brother a settlement, especially Summer as the toy designer, whose designs were no longer her own and were now mass-produced from Taiwan instead of handmade in America like Mr. Anderson had always done. "I'm sorry," he finally managed.

"Sorry for what? Being a money-grubber and ruining my lifestyle, or lying to me and making me fall for you?"

"Both," he muttered. Yet she had fallen for him. Was there hope? He focused on her and saw her chest rise and fall in quick little bursts. Anger, or did she actually care for him? He took a step closer. "I'm sorry, Summer. I'll say it a million times if it helps. Would you ever forgive me?"

She stood her ground. Her eyes narrowed and she clenched her fists. Bringing both hands up, she punched at his chest. Chance reflexively took a step back.

"No!" she yelled. "I'm never going to forgive you. You'd better keep your money-grubbing paws away from me or I will ... spray you with Mace. Ah! I'm so ticked I can't even think of a good threat. Just stay away from me!"

Chance sensed movement behind him. He whirled to see Trevor standing there, luckily minus the gun, but his expression was menacing enough without it. "I think it's time for you to go, son."

Chance glanced back at Summer. "I'm sorry," he muttered weakly.

She shook her head and glared at him, a single tear trickling down her cheek. She brushed it angrily away.

Trevor grabbed his arm. "I told you not to hurt my girl and you did. Get off my property."

Chance felt like he was giving up on Summer, but one more look at her face told him he was getting nowhere tonight. Lead settled in his stomach. He didn't know if he was ever going to penetrate that anger and resentment. Shaking his arm free of Trevor's grasp, he stormed to his sport utility and slammed the door. As he drove away, he made the mistake of glancing back. Trevor had an arm around Summer. She leaned heavily into the older man, and tears streaked down her cheeks.

Those tears almost made him stop, but he didn't hold out much hope that he'd ever be anything but the villain to her.

CHAPTER THIRTEEN

Saturday afternoon, Summer sat behind the desk at Sugar 'n' Spice. It was weird, but such a relief that this was her last day at the shop. She was more than ready to be working in her field. She'd only been in Crested Butte for a little over a month, but she'd come to love the beautiful valley and especially the people. She'd hardly seen Cal, Haley, and Taz, but she loved being around MacKenzie, Isaac, and especially Trevor. Watching him chase Chance off yesterday had warmed her heart, even though part of her had felt bad for Chance. She'd thought he was such a great guy until she realized who he really was. Could he still be a good guy, yet sell people out for a living?

Forcing out a long breath, she wished she could force Chance from her mind as easily as she forced the carbon dioxide from her lungs. Monday morning, she would fly out to meet Marissa and start her new life in Ohio. She hadn't told anyone that she was relocating, and Marissa had been great about her working from wherever she wanted, but it was time for a fresh start. She couldn't handle being here and thinking about Chance, or risk running into him. It was too hard.

She'd thought about not taking the job since Chance obviously gave her the in, but that would be stupid. She needed this job, this opportunity to create her toys and work with a great company. Maybe someday she'd rejoin her friend, Taylor, and her new husband, Lane, and start having adventures she loved again, but for the time being she just wanted to work and feel settled somewhere.

The door clanked open and she automatically called out, "Welcome to Sugar 'n' Spice."

A man swaggered in. For a second, Summer's heart caught. Chance. But then she realized the man was a little taller than Chance, his hair was longer on top, more styled, and his eyes were dark brown instead of the beautiful blue-green she'd come to love on Chance. They could be brothers, though. She shook her head. No, it couldn't be. Chance's brother was in North Carolina.

The man approached the desk, smiling at her.

"Can I help you?" she managed to get out, feeling increasingly uncomfortable.

He nodded and kept coming until he was in her personal space. Summer stood and backed around the desk. "I think you can," he said. His grin broadened, and she noticed he didn't have Chance's dimple.

"Are you Byron?" she couldn't help but ask.

"Yes." His eyes sparkled. "Did my reputation precede me?"

"A wealthy womanizer?"

His smile faltered for half a second, but then a mischievous gleam came in his eyes. "Aw, I'm wounded. That's not really what my brother tells his girl about me."

"I'm not his girl." She jutted out her chin.

"That's a pity. If anyone deserves a girl as beautiful as you, it's Chance."

"You're both scum as far as I'm concerned." Summer tucked her arms across her chest and tilted her head confidently.

"Ouch. What did we do to deserve that?"

"Just being yourselves." She inhaled and forced a snarky smile. "Forcing my dad to sell his company to the highest bidder, who fired me and stole my designs."

"I'm unbelievably sorry the deal didn't go as planned. Sometimes the little people get hurt, but we never intend for that to happen."

"Thanks. So condescending and dismissive." She tapped her fingers on her arm. This guy had a skewed sense of right and wrong. "Plus, I love being referred to as 'the little people.'"

Byron chuckled. "You know I didn't mean it like that, but I do like your spice. Summer, please. Give my brother another chance. He's one of the best guys I know, and he really is crazy about you, like old-time romance movies kind of crazy. I flew in last night to make things right, but I couldn't stand to be around him at the rental house moping anymore." He laughed easily, like they were sharing a great joke as friends.

Summer didn't know what to think about any of Byron's words. Of course his brother would try to defend him, but had Chance really told his brother that he was smitten with Summer?

"I can see by the look in your eyes that you're considering it."

Summer stomped from behind the desk and yanked the front door open, her hand trembling on the handle. "Not even for a second. Don't let the door hit you in the butt on the way out."

Byron approached her with a gleam in his eye. "You're feisty. I really do like that, but you're breaking my brother's heart and that's unacceptable." He rested a hand above her on the doorframe, and it reminded her of Chance doing the same thing. When Chance had done it, she'd wanted a kiss. She just wanted to boot this guy out and never see him again. "You're going to at least talk to my brother or I'll convince Marissa that her new toy designer will never work out."

Summer's breath caught. "Why would Marissa listen to you?"

"We've been friends for years. She trusts me."

"Her loss," Summer spit out.

"You *know* who got you your job." Byron leaned closer. "So what's it going to be, Summer? You can have the job and the guy, and we all live happily ever after." He glanced around the shop. "Or you can keep working as a shop girl."

Summer bit her cheek to keep from screaming at him. How dare he threaten her?

Byron chuckled and brushed some hair from her cheek. She shivered from his unwanted touch. "I'm not saying you have to marry him, Summer, just give him a chance to talk to you."

Byron was yanked away from her, spun around, and had a fist in his jaw before Summer could do more than gasp.

"Stay away from her!" Chance yelled, knocking his brother to the ground with a second hard punch.

Summer jumped back, her hand flying to her mouth as the door swung closed. She'd never imagined Chance could look so scary, but at the same time protective of her. It warmed her, even though she didn't want to experience any good feelings toward this man.

Byron scowled up at him. "Dude, have you lost it?"

Chance glanced over at Summer. His blue-green eyes penetrated into her heart that she thought had cooled of any affection toward him. "I love her."

Summer's breath hitched and the world tilted.

"And you've ruined every hope I had of being with the right woman for me." Chance's voice caught and he cleared his throat, glancing away from Summer. "She's not one of your empty-brained bimbos, Byron. She *is* soul mate material." His broad shoulders heaved from the emotion as he focused on her again.

Summer couldn't hold his gaze, and no matter how much she wanted to, she couldn't be his soul mate. She side-stepped away from him.

Byron climbed to his feet and put his arm around Chance. "Hey, I'm sorry. I wasn't hitting on her. I was trying to help." He glanced back at Summer for reaffirmation.

"Your version of helping is sorely twisted," Summer spit out at him.

Byron winced. "Hey, I'm sorry if it didn't come out right, but you need to listen to Chance. If you had any idea how good of a man my brother is, you wouldn't hesitate for one second to be with him."

Chance gave his brother a forced smile. "Thanks."

They both looked at Summer. She was sorely tempted to at least talk to Chance, especially with those blue-green eyes beseeching her. Instead, she retreated another step. "I'm sorry, but I can't ..." She shook her head. "It's just too hard. You lied to me." She tripped as she tried to rush away while moving backward, hitting the wood floor with a thump and barely catching herself with her hands. Her palms stung, but her pride took a worse hit.

Chance was there before she could stand up. He wrapped an arm around her and helped her to her feet. Summer felt warm all over from his touch and the look in his eyes, but the betrayal over him being the man who'd wrecked her family's business, her creative outlet, and her lifestyle, and then lying to her about it wasn't going to abate.

"Please, Summer," he whispered roughly, pulling her in closer. "Please forgive me."

Summer clung to him for a few wonderful seconds, but then a sob worked its way up her throat as it all crashed around her again. Why did he have to be Mumford's Sons? "I can't." She ripped from his arms and ran to the storage room, locking the door behind her. Leaning against the metal door, she sank to her rear and let the tears roll.

Byron waited for Chance with the most sympathetic expression he'd ever seen on his brother's face. He hated it worse than any of the smug and cocky looks he'd become accustomed to throughout the years.

"Sorry, bro." Byron wrapped an arm around his shoulders again. "Come on. I'll buy you dinner."

"Not hungry," Chance mumbled.

"I know, but it'll get better, I promise."

"Like you've ever had your heart broken."

Byron tilted his head and studied him. "I never told you about why Marissa from KJ's Fun Zone is such a good friend?"

"She broke up with you?"

"The one and only time it's happened. It hurt." Byron's lips tugged down, but almost instantly he seemed to shake it off and his smug expression returned.

"And she's the only one you stayed friends with?"

"You gotta respect a woman who could reel me in and dump me before I had the chance to end it, right?"

"I guess so." Chance was miserable. Absolutely. He may never get Summer back. But for some reason it did help that his brother was here by his side, especially when he noticed Byron's jaw swelling. Punching him had helped a lot too.

CHAPTER FOURTEEN

SUMMER FELL INTO HER NEW WORK AND ROUTINE QUICKLY. SHE couldn't say she was ecstatically happy, but she was fulfilled, and Hudson, Ohio, was a beautiful town with a classic downtown that she enjoyed walking around after work each day. There were lots of trees, but no mountains. She missed the majestic rising mountains of Crested Butte. She missed a whole lot more in Crested Butte, but wouldn't let herself think about that.

Her phone rang as she left her apartment for her nightly walk downtown. Maybe she'd buy herself a cookie from Great Lakes Baking Company and then go sit in the gazebo on the green and watch people go by. Or maybe a brownie instead.

"Hi, Dad," she said.

"How's the new job, sweetheart?"

"I love it." She strolled slowly along, in no real hurry. She didn't have any friends here or any huge rush for anything. She'd sketched and worked on so many different designs on her laptop over the month she didn't have a designing job that she'd spent most of her first two weeks just working with the design and production teams to sort through and implement what she already had ready to go.

"I got an interesting call today from my friend, Byron Judd."

Summer stopped walking in the middle of an intersection. A car honked, and she rushed to the other side of the street, where she leaned against a light pole for support. "Your *friend* Byron Judd?"

"He told me an interesting tale about my beautiful daughter and his brother. I guess Chance is so heartbroken he's making Byron nuts." Her dad chuckled.

"This is not some funny story, Dad. Mumford's Sons ruined your company and my lifestyle. How can you think of either of those two as friends?"

"Sweetheart, you don't know what you're talking about."

"Yes, I do." She unsteadily walked to a bench and sank into it.

"You weren't even in the country when the deal went down," he reminded her.

"All I know is one day I have my dream job designing toys from my laptop, making fabulous money, and traveling the world. Then you partner up with those two jokers and my life is in the crapper."

"They helped me sell my business for much more than I could've dreamed. Usually companies like the one owned by those 'two jokers' buy companies outright, take them apart, and sell them. But Byron and Chance are different. They helped me through the entire process, built my company up, and made it so I sold for twenty million more than I expected to clear, and that's after their fifteen-million-dollar fee."

"Fifteen million?" she stuttered out. Chance had said five.

"Because of them I have my dream retirement, and your mother and I can travel to all those spots you've told us about."

"What about Jake?"

"Byron is the one who recommended Jake to iFrogz. He's doing great. He wouldn't have wanted to keep working for the new owner of Magical Dreams, and neither would you."

"Yeah, but they stole my designs." *My Mini-Me Dolls.* She'd loved those stinking dolls.

"That was unfortunate. Chance wanted to go after them, but there wasn't a lot of legal recourse. We did sign over the designs as part of the deal with Lillywhite."

"I know." She sighed.

"Can I be honest with you, sweetheart?"

She wanted to say no, but she muttered, "I guess."

"You're one of the best toy designers I've ever worked with. Lilly-white would've been smart to keep you on staff, but I was relieved when he let you go. You would've butted heads with him about not being American-made, not using natural products, overcharging for the toys. Most of his philosophies and practices would've rubbed you wrong. You know what I'm saying is true."

Summer didn't respond because he was right. Mr. Lillywhite wasn't her idea of an ideal boss, and she was very grateful to be with Marissa and KJ's Fun Zone now.

"I knew that you would land on your feet, and I was glad you had some savings to give you time to get there," her dad continued.

She winced at that. She'd burned through money quickly traveling the world, but her dad didn't know she hadn't ever looked ahead. She was saving some now and had negotiated royalties on her toys as well. It was comforting to know she wouldn't have to work as a clerk again, even if she lost her job.

"You always have some new idea, so I knew you could be successful on your own," her dad said. "But I also knew it was time for you to stop living the privileged wanderer life and find a way to settle down. Maybe this is the wakeup call you needed."

Summer's temper flared. "I'm an adult, Dad. I think I can decide when I'm ready to grow roots."

"That's true, but I love you, sweetheart, and sometimes when you love someone you have to realize when it's time for them to go through something hard, no matter how difficult it is to watch."

Summer sucked in a breath. She didn't like her dad's words, but she could recognize the truth in them, all of them. She hadn't been around when the buyout had happened, so how did she know that Chance and Byron were some money-suckers? And though she hadn't wanted to settle down, she felt like she'd grown more in the past two months than she had in the years previous, even with all the amazing experiences she'd had. She could be objective enough to realize that she'd never had to be responsible for much. "I love you, Dad."

"No response to any of this, though?"

"I need some time to process."

"I understand. I love you too."

Summer hung up her phone and stared out at the cars crawling along Main Street, not sure if she was growing up or not. A grownup would forgive Chance and be on the next plane to Crested Butte, but she still wasn't sure how to let all her frustrations go that quickly. She sighed and stood. A cookie *and* a brownie from the Great Lakes Baking Company were definitely in order tonight.

CHAPTER FIFTEEN

CHANCE WAITED FOR BYRON TO CREST THE HILL. HIS BROTHER grinned, pedaling past him and whooping as they descended. It was bittersweet to be on a bike ride in the beautiful mountains surrounding Crested Butte and not be with Summer. He thought he'd savored every minute with her, but it wasn't close to enough. He stared at the few pictures he'd taken of her on his cell phone far too often.

Luckily, Byron had stayed with him the past two weeks and they'd had a good time together, working through projects remotely, mountain biking, and talking like they never had. Byron admitted to him that he'd fallen in love with Marissa Yates, Summer's new boss, but she'd broken his heart, run from him, and never explained why. It explained why his brother burned through so many women, but Chance had no clue how to help him either get over Marissa or make her give him a chance. Chance was in a worse situation with the woman he loved.

Byron stopped at the top of the next hill. "Hey. I just got a text from Summer's dad."

"Excuse me?" Chance was already out of breath from the climb, but now he was hyperventilating. "You've been talking to him?"

"Yeah. I called and explained the whole situation." Byron grinned at him. "Even though you don't deserve Summer, I figured I should get in the middle of it."

"And?" Chance wanted to grab him and shake him. He couldn't handle being teased right now.

"He said he'd talk to her."

"And the text said ...?"

"He talked to her. He thinks there might be a possibility of her softening."

Chance stared at his brother for a few seconds, then let out a whoop and pedaled down the hill.

"A small possibility," Byron yelled at him.

"You better keep up or I'm taking the Land Rover and you're riding all the way back to the house," Chance called back.

Byron's loud laughter chased him down the hill. Chance had never been so happy to have a brother.

CHAPTER SIXTEEN

Summer came out of the industrial building of KJ's Fun Zone and headed for her car. It was a muggy day and she only wanted to go home, put on a swimsuit, and climb into the pool at her apartment complex. She crossed the parking lot, but came up short when she saw a man leaning against her Nissan Altima. Her eyes widened and her heart thundered in her chest.

"Chance?" she whispered. It had been two long weeks since she'd seen him, and he looked even better than her memories. She'd cursed herself many a time for not taking pictures of the two of them on her phone. Luckily, there were some shots of him on Google that had helped satiate her when she got missing him too much. His fault for being so wealthy and good-looking.

He straightened when he saw her, but didn't come toward her. Summer gritted her teeth. Was he really going to make her cross the distance? She'd gradually forgiven him for his role in her losing her job —it was impossible not to, after what her dad had revealed to her—but he'd still lied to her. If she was honest with herself and reversed the roles, she probably would've hidden her identity too. There would've been no opportunity to get to know each other otherwise. She could find it in herself to forgive him, but she hadn't been humble or brave enough to go find him. Now he'd come to her. How should she react?

She steeled her spine and stomped toward the car, preparing herself to deal with him without flinging herself into his arms. Clicking the unlock button, she was twenty feet away and doing everything in her power not to look at him when she heard one of her favorite songs by none other than Mumford & Sons. Should've figured he loved them, too, with a business name like that.

Summer's steps faltered and she focused on Chance. He was singing along to the words, which was kind of dorky and absolutely adorable.

"'These days of dust,'" he belted out, "'which we've known, will blow away with this new sun.'"

Summer's heart expanded. Would these awful days of being apart really blow away? Could she let them?

He kept singing about kneeling down and waiting, and he actually did kneel down. Summer couldn't catch a full breath. He was kneeling before her and holding out a hand, and how could she turn him down?

The chorus played, and Chance sang out how he would wait for her.

Summer hadn't been able to cross the distance and reach for his hand. She wanted to, but uncertainty and pain held her away, and she stood melded to the hot asphalt.

Chance got to his feet and more softly sang the next verse, taking a step closer to her. The words were all about forgiving and forgetting. Could she forgive? Would Chance wait for her until she did? As he continued to sing that he would wait for her, she knew he really would. He loved her and would wait as long as it took for her to come to him.

Summer's heart melted and she couldn't take being apart from him any longer. She rushed across the distance and flung herself into his arms. The song kept playing, but she could only focus on Chance's smile growing, and that dimple that she'd missed more than anything else from the beautiful valley of Crested Butte.

He simply held her close, then pulled back and whispered, "Can you please forgive me?"

Summer solemnly nodded her head. "If you promise never to lie to me again."

"That's a deal."

"And you promise to kiss me at least ten times a day."

"Ten?" Chance chuckled. "I was thinking more like twenty."

Summer stood on tiptoe and tasted those lips she'd been daydreaming about for two weeks. The song ended, but their kiss continued. Finally, she pulled back for a breath of air.

Chance kept her in the circle of his arms. "I've got a proposition for you, Summer Anderson."

"Oh, really? I'm listening."

"I talked to your boss."

"Ah! Going behind my back again."

He grinned and continued, "She said you're amazing and feels you could work from anywhere."

Summer's stomach took flight. Was he really going for it?

"So what do you think about Charlotte, North Carolina, in the wintertime, and Crested Butte, Colorado, in the summer? Plus, we can travel anywhere you like. I really want to see Costa Rica and—"

Summer didn't let him finish, kissing him again until she was sure he knew that she approved of the plan.

"Is that a yes?" Chance whispered against her lips.

"If that wasn't a clear enough yes, I might have to repeat the action."

"Yes, please."

His dimple about killed her and she wanted to keep looking at his handsome face, but Summer sacrificed, closed her eyes, and proceeded to tell him yes nonverbally. She didn't plan to stop until they were experts at nonverbal communication.

FREE BOOK

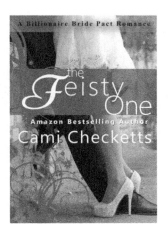

Get your FREE book, *The Feisty One*, from the bestselling Billionaire Bride Pact series, by signing up to be part of my VIP club HERE!

Thank you for reading *The Daring One*. If you enjoyed Chance and Summer's story, you might also enjoy Byron and Marissa's story in *The Disenchanted One*, keep reading, your free copy of this fun, short companion novel to the Billionaire Bride Pact Romances is included.

THE DISENCHANTED ONE: A BILLIONAIRE BRIDE PACT ROMANCE BY CAMI CHECKETTS

CHAPTER ONE

Marissa Yates picked her way around the grassy plateau in her heels. The beautiful setting was hidden in the mountains above the main ski resort of Crested Butte, Colorado. The mountainous town, valley, and especially this secluded wedding spot, were breathtaking. She loved the majestic peaks and all the pine and aspen trees. They had a lot of green back home in Canton, Ohio, but not the looming crests that were so high at the top they were actually above the tree line and it was just gray rock. The contrast was fabulous. She also loved Crested Butte's small downtown area that she'd walked around last night after she'd flown into Gunnison, rented a car, and found the Elevation Hotel and Spa next to the ski resort.

Marissa still had no idea how her adorable toy designer, Summer Anderson, had talked her into coming across the country for Summer and Chance Judd's wedding. She and Summer had become close friends over the past nine months and as CEO of KJ's Fun Zone, Marissa had never been happier with the innovative designs coming out of production. Yet being at this wedding was asking more of Marissa than even her professional façade could handle.

Of course, she hadn't confided in Summer about her worries of seeing Byron Judd for the first time in three years. Summer assumed her future husband's brother and her new boss were friends. Byron had, after all, gotten Summer the job with Marissa. She and Byron *were* friends, mostly because he insisted on keeping in contact. Yet how could you truly be friends with the only man you'd ever loved? A man who was certain to break your heart into a thousand pieces if you let him close again?

Luckily, she hadn't seen Byron last night. He'd texted to see if she'd gotten into town all right, and asked if they could get together for dinner. She'd begged exhaustion and he'd been gracious enough to allow her the excuse. The man's charm had no end. If only it hadn't worked on every woman in the world, charming the pants off of any attractive female that came within a hundred miles of him.

Okay, that was an exaggeration. He'd been a gentleman when she'd dated him, and he probably only charmed his adoring female crowd out of kisses. Her face heated as she remembered his lingering and all-encompassing kiss. The way he'd treated her like she was the only woman for him. Three years and she still couldn't forget. He'd probably dated a couple thousand women since then while she'd married herself to her job and risen to be one of the youngest and most successful female CEO's in the nation. Head hunters approached her constantly, trying to woo her to different companies, but she loved KJ's Fun Zone with all her heart. It was like her first-born child, and she couldn't imagine ever leaving it. Thank heavens her work sort of filled the emptiness only Byron could satiate.

Guests were filing in and taking their seats. Marissa recognized some of them from the tabloids—NHL star Beckham Taylor and his exotic-looking artist wife, Alyssa. Then she noticed billionaire creator of Friend Zone, Tucker Shaffer, and his petite, blonde wife. She couldn't remember her name, but she was a beautiful lady. She grinned over at Marissa like they were the best of friends. Marissa was tempted to go introduce herself and see if she could sit with them when *he* appeared in her vision.

She saw him first and was able to admire the way his tall, well-built frame filled out a tailored suit before his dark eyes focused in on her as if she were the only woman in the world. Byron Judd's eyes lit up and he walked toward her with panther-like grace. When he flashed that smile at her, the years since she'd seen him melted away. The only thing she wanted was to be in his arms again, and have him tell her she was the one he wanted to be with.

Yet it had all been lies. The night after he'd confided his love to her, she'd found him hugging and kissing another woman. Marissa had run away from his office, North Carolina, and any hope of a relationship, without telling him what she'd seen, only that they were never going to work as a couple. A woman did have her pride. They'd maintained a friendship, but only because Byron had insisted on calling, texting, and emailing every few days. He always made her laugh, but she'd stayed strong and hadn't seen him these long, lonely years. Her spine straightened. She knew he hadn't been lonely. She'd seen pictures of him online with woman after woman, and her college friends from North Carolina confirmed that he blew through women faster than designer suits.

He reached her and she straightened her spine, tilted her chin up, and extended her hand.

"Oh, no," Byron chuckled. "I haven't seen you in three years and you think you're getting away with a handshake?"

Marissa swallowed and didn't have any response. Byron wrapped his arms around her and she felt like she'd come home. He smelled insanely good. A Tom Ford cologne, if she had to guess—a citrus, musk, and vanilla blend. His muscled chest pressed against her was enough to drive her crazy. It was all she could do to not lift up her head and see if his kiss was as intoxicating as his smell and her memories.

When she did lift her head, Byron was staring at her with a hunger that made her breath catch. His eyes flickered to her lips then back to her eyes. "Ah, Marissa, you still have the power to make me want to commit myself to you for the eternities."

She pulled back. "Nobody has that power, I'm afraid."

Byron pumped his eyebrows. "Wouldn't it be worth trying, though?"

"Trying what?" She looked sharply at him. How dare he claim he could commit to anyone for longer than a month?

"Trying out my lips?" His tongue darted over said lips and they looked more than worth a sample. "For old time's sake?"

Marissa's heart must've stopped or this stinking high altitude was killing her. She couldn't catch a full breath and she was getting lightheaded.

Chance approached, looking handsome in his tux and a little nervous. He tugged on Byron's sleeve. "It's time, bro." He gave Marissa a quick hug. "Great to see you. Thanks for coming."

"I wouldn't miss it."

Chance hurried away, still gripping his brother. Byron gave her one last look like a cat ready to devour the mouse. Marissa closed her eyes and clutched at the neck of her silky, white blouse. She could not allow herself to be the mouse again. Byron would have to survive on the gourmet cat food he'd devoured for the past three years.

Byron tried to keep his eyes on his brother's golden-haired bride as she practically pranced down the aisle, but he could not keep his gaze from straying to Summer's exquisite boss. Marissa Yates had cut his heart out and stomped on it three years ago, but for some reason he could not cut her loose. After too much chasing and begging on his part as to what had gone wrong, he'd finally agreed to stop asking and to her terms of friendship, completely befuddled by the request.

Yes, he was secure in his looks and charm, and it never hurt that he was insanely wealthy. Women came to *him* and he used to enjoy every minute of the different flings, but no woman had touched him or broken him like Marissa. He often wondered if he couldn't forget her because she'd been the one to end it. The theory made sense, but he swore there was something more. The substance and depth that Marissa exhibited, he'd always wanted to hold onto. He'd never found her equal in another woman.

Studying her as she focused on the bride, all the longing he'd tried to bury for two years and then used as his motivation the past seven months to make a change and be worthy of her, hit him again—the delicate yet strong form, the silky mahogany hair, the high cheekbones, large pale blue eyes, and bow-shaped lips that he wanted to claim as his own.

She caught him looking at her and gave him a quick smile before focusing on the wedding couple. Was it his imagination, or was she as affected by seeing him again as he was? A man could hope for a miracle.

The preacher must've said man and wife because Chance and Summer were kissing, and everyone was cheering. Byron smiled and cheered along with everyone else, needing to stay in the moment. This was his brother's big day, and Chance deserved every happiness in the world. Byron wished he could find a love like Chance and Summer, but the only woman who fit that bill for him had dumped him, and from the way she extended her hand all formal-like when he saw her, he didn't think getting back into her good graces was going to be as easy as he'd hoped.

Summer kept telling him that Marissa's face lit up when she talked about him and she still thought there was a chance. He and Summer had spent a lot of time the past seven months plotting how to get Marissa to the wedding, and make Byron's play for her foolproof. Summer liked to call it "The Lonely Billionaire Pact". His brother's new wife loved to tease.

The bride and groom didn't walk back down the aisle, but stayed in place and started hugging everyone around them, while still clinging to each other's hands.

Byron thumped his brother on the back. "I'm thrilled for you, bro. Summer's perfect for you."

"Thanks." Chance grinned. "Love you."

"You too." Byron found himself getting a little choked up. His brother was the best man he knew, and Byron would do anything for him.

Summer stretched up and hugged him, interrupting his congrats with, "Lonely Billionaire Pact is in place. You're seated next to Marissa at dinner."

Byron pulled back and smiled. His brother's new wife truly was a doll. "Oh, yeah?"

"Oh, *yeah*." Summer gave him a wink and then was swept away to the next group for congratulations. One of the girls was squealing something about hardly seeing each other since summer camp at Wallakee, and how happy they were that Summer had kept "the pact." Summer had told him about her and her friends Billionaire Bride Pact and how she never planned on keeping it until she fell for Chance.

Another one of Summer's friends was a teeny blonde, dwarfed by her massive husband, Byron thought he was creator of Friend Zone. The blonde was bouncing in excitement over Summer's dress and the gorgeous setting for the wedding. Byron smiled. He loved women and their enthusiasm. Thinking of women, it was past time he found Marissa again. She'd resisted every attempt he'd made to see her in person the past three years. He'd drawn up plans of attack on several different occasions, intending to show up at her work and sweep her off her feet, but when a woman kept telling you no, you respected that. He might only have today to win her over to Team Judd. He needed to take advantage of every minute.

CHAPTER TWO

Instead of rushing up to congratulate the bride and groom, Marissa tried to find a way to disappear. The problem was, the wedding party had all ridden up to the picturesque valley in four-wheel drive vehicles because of the muddy terrain. She walked over to where they were parked to inquire if there was anyone available to take her back to town, and there was no one around. She finally found a driver, but he was helping carry food to the buffet table.

"I need a ride back into town," she said in her professional tone. "I can pay whatever is necessary." She softened her voice, "Please."

"Sorry, ma'am. No one's going back down until after the dinner. I'm under contract to help here. Unless it's an emergency."

Oh, she wished she could lie and say it was an emergency, but was that fair to pull this guy away from his job? She appreciated dedicated employees. Yet, this was an emergency of the heart. If she didn't get away, Byron might find her again, and she'd barely survived the thirty seconds of interaction before the ceremony. What if he had a full five minutes? He'd convince her to not only kiss him, but declare her love for him. Five minutes later, she'd see him off wooing some pretty girl from the wedding party. No. She wasn't having any of it.

A firm hand on her back yanked her from her nightmarish visions of the man she loved in the arms of another woman.

Byron was glancing over her with concern. "Riss? You okay, love?"

How did he do that? His pet name for her *and* a term of endearment, coupled with worry in those dark eyes, and she was faltering faster than her spotty cell service up this mountain.

"Fine, thank you." She jerked from his touch and strode back toward the wedding party. More people. That would be the key to keeping him at an un-kissable distance.

Byron was at her side, with his arm around her waist, before she could react. She felt like the air had been knocked out of her. That manly hand placed possessively on her hip. His tall frame holding her close. The luxurious scent of his cologne. It was too much and was completely unfair of him.

"I've missed you all these years," he murmured close to her ear.

Marissa glanced sharply at him, and unfortunately his lips brushed along her cheek before she could draw back. Her breath was coming in short pants. She wished she could throw a comeback about how he'd never come to see her, but she knew he had and she'd hidden from him. She'd stayed stronger than a mule, even though sometimes she felt as stupid as one, turning down the most charming man on the planet over and over again.

Byron stopped and pulled her around to face him. "You're the only woman who could ever do this to me."

"Do what?"

His eyes swept over her face. "Make me insane waiting for you."

He grinned and she realized how completely and horribly she'd missed him. Why had she kept her distance? Was it really worth not being near this man when she loved him so desperately? Then what he'd said really and truly sunk into her thick, twitterpated brain. She was only another game to him. A challenge. She made him wait so he pursued. It was his life quest to have every woman fall at his feet.

"You can wait until eternity, but it won't matter," she snapped at him.

The ache in his eyes made her regret her words instantly. Byron blinked and his arms dropped away from her.

"I'm sorry," she whispered, hating that she'd hurt him. Even if he was the biggest player in the dating game, he was her friend, and she didn't want to cause him pain. "Can we just ... be friends? We've done a pretty good job with that over the past three years."

Byron's lips recovered their smile but not his eyes. "Of course." He offered her his arm and she slipped her hand through, hoping she could handle being close to him without doing or saying something she'd regret. Like admitting that if he really was waiting for her, she'd commit herself to him for eternity and beyond. She shook her head. It would never happen.

"What's going on in that brilliant brain?" Byron asked.

"Nothing," she said quickly.

He chuckled. "Now, I don't believe that. If you're not scheming how to up production or beat out the competition, you're daydreaming about me."

She shook her head and bit at her lip. How did he know how much she thought about him?

"Seeing you again." He smiled and lowered his voice, "You're more exquisite than any scenery I've viewed from Thailand to New Zealand."

"Thank you." She blushed, but held her head high and tried to take the compliment graciously. What was it about this man that made her forget she was a confident, business professional?

Byron escorted her to a side table where they had a good view of the bride, groom, his parents, and Summer's parents, but they had a measure of privacy too. The wedding party was all celebrating, talking, and starting on their salads as Byron and Marissa took their assigned seats. It was awkward that she was right up front like she was part of the family, or Byron's date, or something.

Byron's parents glanced over at her. His mom whispered something to his dad then they both stared and smiled some more. She'd been forced to fire employees and not felt as uncomfortable as she did at this moment.

Marissa managed what she hoped was her confident smile, took a sip of her water, then focused on her salad. The dressing was tangy and rich, a creamy poppy seed and she loved the strawberry-spinach salad's crunchy sweetness. She enjoyed a few bites uninterrupted, grateful she could eat at all with Byron nearby.

His knee rubbed against hers and the bite of spinach stuck in her throat. She swallowed then glanced up. Their gazes met and tangled, an entire conversation passed between them, almost without her permission. The earnestness and warmth of his look was a dagger through her abdomen. How could she still love him so much? She knew who he was, what he was. He wasn't future husband material and never would be. When he was eighty he'd still be smoking hot and still have women crawling all over him.

The waitress came to request their drink orders. She nodded to Marissa's request of a lemon for her water and fawned all over Byron as he ordered lemonade.

"She's interested, you realize that?" Marissa couldn't help but fling at Byron.

His eyes broke concentration on her face for half a second as he glanced at the retreating young thing then he focused back on her and it was a wonder Marissa could breathe at all.

"Was she?" He reached for her hand under the table, rubbing his thumb along it.

"It happens so often you don't even notice anymore?" She should pull her hand away to safety, but it felt too good.

Byron's dark eyes sparkled. "The jealous look is a good one on you, but then everything looks good on you."

Marissa sputtered for a response, but couldn't come up with one.

"You're the epitome of successful, classy, and beautiful—the long, shiny, dark hair, the absolutely gorgeous face and toned body that looks fabulous in those pencil skirts. But it's your goodness and beauty inside that is the reason I'm devoted to you for life, Riss."

"Nobody calls me Riss but you." Devoted for life? Why couldn't he have said those words in his usual teasing tone? She was free-falling into his romantic gorge of death. How to catch herself?

"Their loss. It fits you."

"And you're never going to commit yourself to one woman, so let's just forget you even suggested it." She pulled her hand back and hoped the sharp comment would give her a safety rope to hold onto and push him back to his side of the cliff.

Byron's eyes reflected a deep sadness, but he didn't complain. The waitress was approaching with a loaded tray. "So the waitress was checking me out, eh?"

She rolled her eyes. "You know she was."

"Doesn't matter." He thanked the waitress as she set their drinks down then he focused back on Marissa. "There's only one woman I want checking me out."

Marissa couldn't hold his gaze. Why was he doing this to her? Three years since he ripped her heart out and she'd stayed strong. She'd built a fabulous life for herself, without him, without any man. Sure she dated, but she never allowed it to get serious. How could Byron yank her back into his looks, and his touches, and the desire to spend every minute with him?

She toyed with another bite of salad, but couldn't force herself to eat anymore. Glancing away from the too-handsome man who was still gazing at her, as if waiting for her to confirm that she was the woman for him, she studied the rest of the wedding party. Besides Summer's friends and their husbands, there were some guests that she could easily pick out as family members of either the groom or the bride. A nice-looking group overall, and everyone seemed to be enjoying themselves. Her eyes caught on a gorgeous brunette who was laughing with the man seated next to her. The recognition was instantaneous for Marissa and it felt like someone had just shoved a hot poker into her abdomen.

The girl glanced over and noticed Marissa staring at her. Her eyes flickered to Byron, of course. She gave a coy smile and a little wave then turned away. Marissa's entire body was rigid. It couldn't be the same girl. Why would she be here? Did Byron invite her? Why was he sitting next to Marissa when the woman he cheated on Marissa with was less than fifty feet away?

"Riss?" Byron touched her hand. "You're freezing, love. Are you all right?"

Marissa closed her eyes. The pain washed over her anew. Byron, whirling that beautiful girl around then holding her close. She'd known in that instant that every rumor about him was true and Marissa wasn't the love of his life, she was just another number. She'd sprinted away from the scene in Byron's office that night, and escaping was the only option for her right now.

She thought she mumbled, "Excuse me," but wasn't sure as she pushed back from the table and walked swiftly away from the wedding party. She ripped off her heels and broke into a run as she passed the trucks they'd rode up in. Within seconds, she was dodging mud puddles and sprinting down the mountain road. It didn't matter that she was barefoot and had no clue how far away her hotel was. She might get lost in these mountains. As long as she was away from that girl, and Byron, she could survive.

"Riss!" Byron caught her much too quickly. He reached for her arm, but she pulled free and ran off the left side of the road, into the thick trees. It was stupid behavior, especially for a city girl, but being mauled by a bear or mountain lion sounded preferable to explaining to Byron why she was reacting so insanely.

Branches scratched at her face and arms. Her blouse snagged and tore. Rocks and twigs pummeled the soles of her feet. She didn't care. She kept running. Her toe caught on a root and she went down, hard. Slamming into the uneven ground, her shoes went flying from her grasp. Her hands took the brunt of the beating, but she scratched up her knees also.

"Marissa!" Byron was there before she could even try to pull herself up. He dropped to his knees beside her. Marissa rolled over with a groan and sat up. She hadn't even realized she was crying until the tears dropped from her chin down to her chest.

"Are you okay?" Byron whispered.

She stared at him. No, she wasn't okay. She'd never be okay without him, but she couldn't tell him that. She shook her head, and tried to push to her feet. Byron wrapped his arms around her, tugging her to him. He sat back against a tree, pulled her onto his lap like a little child, and simply held her. It was too much. Marissa didn't fight the tears anymore. Three years of missing him, and denying that she wanted him, and now here he was, holding her. With that woman who had torn them apart half a mile away, eating salad and wondering where her boyfriend had gone. Marissa barked a harsh laugh. That woman probably had no more hold on Byron than Marissa did. He'd most likely been with hundreds of women in the past three years.

Byron pulled back and stared at her. "You're scaring me, love. What's going on?"

Marissa shook her head and blew out her breath. "Please stop calling me love. We both know it's not true."

Byron blinked at her. "Riss. If you would only believe me. You're the only woman I've ever wanted to call love."

"Ha!" She tried to break free from his grasp, but he was too strong. "Let me go."

"If you want me to, I will, but, please, please don't want me to, Riss." He relaxed his hold and brushed a hand through her hair, dislodging some twigs. He picked them out and smiled gently at her. "Three years. Three long years I've wanted to see you, hold you, talk about why you ran from me, but you would never let me. Please don't run away now. I can't wait another three years to see you again."

His words were so tender, so heartfelt, she broke down again. The tears came in a rush and they clogged up her throat and made it impossible to respond to him. She buried her face in his suitcoat and sobbed. Part of her knew she needed to get it together. Byron probably thought she was insane and she looked the opposite of a professional.

Yet she needed this cry almost as much as she needed him. She was ruining his suitcoat and he wouldn't want to see her for at least three years after this display of emotion, but his hands rubbing against her silky shirt, sitting on his lap like this, it was a dream come true and nightmarish anguish at the same time. She'd missed him like she could never describe and as soon as he let her go, she'd never see him again. She couldn't handle ever seeing him again.

Finally, she got a grip and pulled back. He was watching her with too much concern in his eyes. "Is all this for me? Have I hurt you, Riss?"

She blinked at him. Had he hurt her? Only every day.

"I would never want to hurt you."

Marissa pulled free and pushed to her feet. Byron stood quickly, and without her heels on, he had her by half a foot. She'd always thought they were the perfect height for each other.

"You have no idea what you're talking about," she muttered. "Every woman is a game to you." She wanted to run, but she held her ground and looked into his eyes. She'd faced down entire board rooms and stood strong in her convictions, she could win against Byron's beseeching eyes. Those dark eyes that usually sparkled with humor and mischief were now very serious as they studied her.

"You've never been a game to me."

She wanted to believe him, everything in her begged her to believe him, but the proof was all there. Every photo on the Internet with a different girl. Every old friend of hers from college, who still lived in Charlotte, informing her about all the women he went through.

"Aargh!" she screamed. "I can't do this with you."

She turned away, but Byron caught her arm and turned her back. "Do what, love? Why can't you give us a chance? Why did you run away from me three years ago and refuse to see me since?"

The years melted away. She'd been finishing her MBA at UNC's business school, Kenan-Flagler's, when a friend introduced her to Byron. The connection had been instantaneous, and she was certain she'd found the love of her life. They only dated a couple of months, but Byron was fun, romantic, smart, successful—everything she'd wanted. She'd been the oldest of ten and her life was focused on working hard, getting the full-ride scholarship, being a good example, and making her parents proud. She loved her family, but had never experienced life like she did with Byron. He made every moment sparkle and shine, and might be the only person who could make her laugh and simply enjoy herself.

It had all crashed down on her the day before she'd graduated. She'd been offered the most amazing job with KJ's Fun Zone. Byron had teased that he wasn't going to let her move to Ohio, but she knew he'd support her and they'd make their relationship work. What they had was too magical to let it go.

She'd had some extra time with classes and finals done, and decided to surprise him at his company, Mumford's Sons. Walking out of the elevator she saw him in the lobby, hugging the breathtaking brunette like he hadn't seen her in a year and was in heaven holding her. The girl smiled up at him so worshipfully then leaned in to kiss him.

Marissa had been warned by many people that he was a player, but she was too gone over him to listen. When the proof smacked her in the face, she'd turned back to the elevator and disappeared from his life. He'd tried time and again to get her to see him. She'd even heard that he'd gone to Canton, Ohio to look for her, but she'd been smart and gone home to Vermont for a few weeks to recoup before she started her new job. She'd been such a mess her saintly mother had actually told a lie for her when Byron showed up on their doorstep. She'd hidden out until she was certain he'd left town.

Could she tell him the reasons now? All these years she'd never told him why she ran, simply that she needed to be friends. He'd begged her to see him, but he'd respected her boundaries, and they'd become good friends through emails, texts, snaps, and phone calls. She loved him more than she could ever admit, but she knew she'd been smart to break it off. Byron could never settle down.

"I didn't run, I needed space."

His dark eyes penetrated through her. "I've given you lots of space."

"I'm sure it was difficult for you, dating a different woman every week."

Byron's eyebrows rose. "Keeping tabs on me, love?"

"That's what friends do," she insisted, folding her arms across her chest, forcing him to release his grip on her forearm. She couldn't handle any more touch from him.

"You've been a good friend to me," he said, his voice low and soothing, "But I need more."

Marissa's heart rate sped up. "Need or want?"

His grin appeared then and she knew she wasn't going to survive this conversation emotionally intact. "Both, love." He took a step closer and although she kept her arms folded, his chest brushed against them, sending off alarms in her head. "I need you close *and* I want you like I've never wanted anyone."

Marissa had to back up. She unclenched her arms and grabbed hold of a tree branch for support. "I'm not one of your little flings, Byron."

"I know that." He nodded. "Believe me. I've learned that lesson well the past three years. The last thing I want from you is a fling."

"What do you want from me?"

He smiled again, but this time it was more gentle. "I want all of you, Marissa. I want you by my side morning, noon, and especially night. I want you today and every day until I die, then I pray a merciful Lord will let me have you by my side in heaven."

Marissa stared at him, her mouth sliding open then closing, she probably looked like a clownfish. Could she believe his speech, any of it? "Byron," she finally whispered. "I fell so hard for you, but you couldn't even be committed to me for a couple of months. How can you claim to want me for life, because I swear I am not sharing you with any other woman." The last few words were said so vehemently she expected him to back up a step. He came closer, gently touching her cheek and causing her to tremble all over.

"I wouldn't even notice another woman if I had you."

"Ha!" She barked out. "You want to know why I ran today, and three years ago?"

"I'd give away my company to know."

Marissa was certain he was exaggerating now. He'd worked harder to build Mumford's Sons with his brother than even she had worked to make KJ's Fun Zone skyrocket. Yet the seriousness in his voice couldn't be denied.

She swallowed and finally admitted, "That perfect little brunette."

Byron's hand dropped and his forehead wrinkled. "*What* brunette?"

Marissa drew a long breath. "Three years ago I came to your office to see you. It was the day before graduation."

He nodded. "You didn't walk at graduation. I had no clue where you'd gone."

"I saw you hugging that brunette. The one who's here today."

"I have no idea ..." His eyes widened and a second later he connected it. "Lucy?"

"I don't know her name." In fact, she wished the girl didn't have a name. It made it all too real and horrible.

"Long, dark hair, small, right? Like five feet nothing?"

Marissa gave a jerky nod.

Byron shook his head and laughed. Why on earth did he laugh? Couldn't he see her pain? He sobered quickly, crossed the distance between them, and cupped her face with his palms. She wanted to pull away, but simply couldn't do it.

"Oh, love. Lucy is my cousin. That day you saw us at the office I hadn't seen her in over a year because she'd been doing volunteer work in South America then went to California for school. I remember picking her up and hugging her because I was so excited to see her, and she probably kissed me, she always does. Chance and I always joke about how we have to turn our heads quick, or she gets us on the lips." He gave a half-laugh again. "She's here for Chance's wedding. What you saw was completely innocent. I swear I never cheated on you and I never would."

Marissa's mind was spinning. His cousin. Oh, my, no! She'd ruined the past three years because she saw him picking up, spinning, and kissing his cousin! She blinked quickly, forcing herself not to cry again. She'd cried enough today, but honestly this was horrible.

"Byron, why didn't you tell me?"

"Tell you?" He gazed at her incredulously. "Riss, I didn't have a clue why you left. I chased after you and couldn't find you in Ohio or Vermont. You kept sending me these messages that you just needed space and then that you just wanted to be friends. I've done everything I could these past three years to break through your wall, and been rebuffed for everything but a 'friend'. What else did you expect me to do?"

A quick breath burst out of her and she did the only thing she could do. She kissed him full on the mouth. He reacted quickly, tucking her into his arms and taking full advantage of her willing mouth. The kiss was as magical and wonderful as she remembered their kisses being. Sunshine and happiness exploded through her as the pressure of his mouth increased.

When she finally pulled back, she was breathing hard. Why had she waited so long for this, for him? They would need to kiss for days to make up for lost time.

Byron was grinning at her. "I love you, Marissa Yates."

She felt the words seep into her. She'd wanted to hear them from him for much too long. "I love you too," she admitted.

He kissed her softly, the aching sweetness of his touch lighting her up from the inside out. His kiss deepened and Marissa savored each movement of his lips. The way his hands held her with strength and tenderness. His smell. All of him.

He gave a low groan and simply held her close. "You don't know how happy you've made me, Riss. How long I've waited to touch you, hold you, tell you that I love you. So many times I've hated myself as I kissed another woman and wanted her to be you, but it never felt like you ..." He stopped and grimaced. "Whoa, sorry. That didn't come out right."

It was the slap in the face Marissa didn't want, but maybe she needed. Oh, reality was not her friend. She backed up and his arms dropped away. Silence stretched between them for a few horrible seconds. Byron swallowed and said, "Riss. You know there have been other women."

"I know and I appreciate you being honest about it." How could she have told him she loved him and simply forgotten about all the past, present, and future women competing for Byron Judd? She was fighting tears again and it ticked her off. She was a professional, successful woman, and yet here she was—scratched up, dirty, teary-eyed, and falling for a man who couldn't stay true to her. It just wasn't in his DNA.

"But there's something I need to tell you," he said.

Marissa held up a hand. "You need to get back to the wedding dinner. I apologize for making you miss so much of your brother's wedding day."

"No, Riss, you need to hear this."

"I ..." She blinked quickly. Byron would never be true to her. He might as well cut her heart out as lie to her that he would try to be faithful. "I can't do this."

Byron opened his mouth, but the rumble of a truck coming down the road grabbed Marissa's attention. She pivoted and ran with everything in her toward the road. She could hear Byron on her heels, but she was fleeing for her sanity. Even though being barefoot hurt, it probably made her faster with gripping the sometimes muddy ground. She heard Byron slip, hit the ground, and curse. Wincing for him, but not willing to stop, she dodged onto the road. The truck almost hit her, brakes squealing and dust exploding from under its tires as it ground to a halt.

Marissa held up a hand and rushed around to the passenger side, yanking the door open and climbing onto the running board. "Can you take me down the mountain?" she begged the middle-aged driver.

He stared at her like she was an alien, but nodded shortly.

Byron ran in front of the truck as she slammed the door shut. "Drive," she screamed.

Byron made it around to her side. She shoved the door lock down before Byron could yank on the handle. The man stared at her, but dropped it into gear and pulled away.

Byron banged on the door and hollered, "Marissa, wait."

The tears were back and Marissa begged the driver. "Please, please, drive."

He pushed the gas down and Marissa hated that she watched out of the side mirror as Byron ran alongside the truck then dropped further and further behind. She closed her eyes as wetness trickled down her face.

"Ain't none of my business," the man said, "but I think that gentleman had something to say to you."

"Nothing he says can change the truth," Marissa muttered.

"Ah, one of those?" He downshifted and the truck slowed on the steep slope.

Marissa could only nod. She was too spent to even wipe the tears away.

CHAPTER THREE

Byron finally admitted to himself he wasn't going to catch the truck speeding away with Marissa, and stopped in the middle of the muddy road. His chest heaved from the exertion and the emotion. Had she really run away from him again? Was he ever going to convince her that he was genuine? That he loved her and only her?

He turned and trudged back to the wedding party. Looking down at his suit, he knew he was in for some teasing from his brother and concerned looks from everyone else. He laughed shortly, trying to remember the last time he'd ruined a tailored suit. Okay, he'd probably never ruined a tailored suit. He tried to brush the mud off his pants, straighten his shirt and coat, and smooth his hair.

He slipped into the wedding party, pasting on a smile he didn't feel. Luckily the dinner was over and people were milling around talking. He got a few questioning looks, but he was able to downplay any questions with his usual charm. His brain was spinning with ways to find Marissa, and yet make Chance's day great. He had to keep reminding himself this day was about Chance and Summer, not him, but it felt like if he didn't find Marissa and tell her everything, she'd slip away and he'd never get another chance.

He greeted family members and met all of Summer's girl's camp friends. It was only when Summer pinned him alone that he got the harsh whisper, "Where is Marissa?"

He forced a smile for onlookers as he wrapped an arm around his new sister-in-law. "I messed it up. She ran again."

Her face crumpled. "No. I was so hoping…"

"It'll all work out," he lied. "I don't want you to worry."

An elderly gentleman, he thought it was Summer's grandpa, was approaching her with arms held out. Summer gave Chance a squeeze. "She's staying at the Elevation Hotel. Go find her quick."

"Got it. Thanks, sis." He pecked her on the cheek and then released her so she could hug her grandpa. Byron smiled when moments later Chance grabbed his wife to start the dancing. Summer was perfect for his brother, and Byron couldn't have been happier for them. He wanted their day to be perfect, but he also wanted to slip away as quickly as possible and find Marissa. He prayed she'd gone back to her hotel and not to the nearest airport.

Marissa slipped out of her ripped clothes, cursing herself for leaving her favorite pair of Manolo Blahnik heels on the muddy mountain. She took a hot shower, and then dressed in a blousy black shirt and patterned tights. She didn't usually dress this casual, but she wanted to be comfy if she had to wait at the airport all day for a flight. Her flight was scheduled for tomorrow afternoon, but she couldn't stay here any longer. Couldn't risk Byron finding her and talking her into staying with him for life. She wished it could be different and she could trust him, but he wasn't going to reform for her. It was too much to hope for.

She glanced around the hotel room, certain she'd packed everything. Shouldering her purse, she dragged her suitcase behind her, out the door, and down the hallway. She'd almost reached the elevator when it dinged open. Byron rushed out, looking impossibly handsome and disheveled. His dress shoes were coated with grime, his suit coat was gone, his white shirt had dirt stains on it, his fitted dress pants had a rip in the leg and mud caked on them, and his hair was mussed. He'd never looked better.

A small gasp escaped and she almost threw herself into his arms and cried with gratitude that he'd found her. She held her ground and the elevator closed behind him. His dark eyes swept over her. She didn't know how to escape, or if she even wanted to.

"Room key, please," he said.

Marissa blinked at him, but pulled the key out of her purse and handed it to him. He nodded, not smiling as he took her suitcase and wrapped his hand around her elbow, escorting her back to her suite as if it was the only option she had. It probably was.

"How'd you know where I was?" she murmured.

"Summer's been my ally in reconnecting us." He unlocked the door and gestured for her to go first.

Marissa walked through and sank wearily into one of the chairs. She couldn't risk the couch and him sitting right beside her. Summer wanted them together? She should've guessed with how insistent her friend was that she be at the wedding, and talking Byron up every chance she got. Summer wouldn't want her with somebody who would break her heart again, would she?

"She knew my room number?"

"The girl at the front desk was very helpful." Byron sat in the chair opposite her, as if guessing that she couldn't handle any physical contact right now.

"Of course she was," Marissa snipped out then instantly regretted it. She pinched at her forehead to try to alleviate the headache that was coming. "Byron, I'm sorry. You know me. You know this isn't normal for me to be crying and bratty, but I really can't do this with you anymore."

He leaned forward and braced his elbows on his powerful thighs. "Listen to me for a few minutes, please. Then if you still want me to leave, I promise ..." He shook his head and cleared his throat. "I promise I'll go and I won't come to you again, unless you ask me to."

Marissa could appreciate what it took for him to say those words. She didn't want him to go either, but they couldn't work as a couple. In his way, Byron did love her, but she wouldn't agree to his version of love. Her, and who knew how many women on the side. Call her old-fashioned, but she wanted a whole, committed relationship like her parents and grandparents had savored throughout their married lives.

"I'll listen," she finally conceded. Byron always kept his word. If she listened and then asked him to leave, this drama would be over, and maybe someday she could heal and move on.

"Thank you." He continued leaning toward her and said, "It about killed me when you disappeared three years ago."

Marissa wanted to respond, but she'd agreed to let him talk.

He stood and paced in the small area in front of her, his movements were strong and sure and she wondered how any woman, herself included, could ever resist him.

"I told you how I searched for you, but when I couldn't find you and then you kept insisting we could only be friends, I flipped out a little bit." He clenched his fists. "I dated any woman who appealed to me, then I tossed them away for the stupidest reasons you can imagine —didn't smell right, didn't talk right, not fun enough, not smart enough, didn't know how to kiss." He ticked off the reasons then stopped in front of her and stared down at her. "Basically none of them were you, none of them came close to you."

Marissa clung to the chair handles to keep herself from rising and going to him. She hated that he'd lost himself in other women to try to find her, but yet he had tried to find her, any way possible.

"Then Chance found Summer." A brief smile flitted over his face and he sank into the chair again and faced her. "I was so happy for them, and as I got to know her and they planned their wedding, she and I became close friends. I confided in both of them how much I loved you and she gave me a challenge. No women. Not so much as a lunch date. No physical contact of any kind, until their wedding day. She promised me she'd get you here and give me a chance with you. She called it our Lonely Billionaire Pact and I have been lonely ... for you." His dark eyes had never been more sincere.

Marissa simply stared at him, trying to comprehend what he was saying. He loved her. He and Summer had planned and schemed to reunite them. But the huge whammy. "You haven't dated any other woman?"

He gave her the full force of his devastating smile. "For two-hundred and seventy-one days."

"Glad it wasn't two-hundred and seventy-two or we would've been sunk." She couldn't hold in the half-laugh. "How did you survive?"

He chuckled. "It wasn't easy at first. Flirting and wooing had become second nature to me, but I controlled myself, and Summer took some pretty great pictures of you for me. Those helped a lot. I'd look at them and read your latest text, or listen to a voice mail from you, and it became very easy to not even look twice at another woman."

Marissa saw him, truly saw him for the first time in three years. He had committed to her, and she hadn't even known it. He loved her like she wanted to be loved. She pushed from her seat and knelt in front of him, grabbing his hands in hers.

Byron's eyebrows leapt up. "Riss?"

"Swear to me it's true. You love me, and only me. You gave up dating other women for seven months to prove it."

"It's true. I swear it on Mumford's Sons and KJ's Fun Zone."

She smiled. His company and her job were the constants they both knew and trusted.

He tugged her up and before she knew it she was sitting on his lap, secure and happy in his arms. He kissed her, softly at first, but then neither of them could hold back and the passion and love he felt for her encompassed her as surely as his arms. He released her mouth and trailed kisses along her jaw then down her neck.

"Stop," Marissa stuttered out.

Byron drew back. "Wh-what?"

Marissa ran her hands through his hair and grinned at him. "You'd better stop or my daddy's going to have to force you to marry me."

Byron chuckled, kissed her until she was floating, and then whispered against her mouth. "I've waited three long years for you, love. Elope with me tonight and I'll take you anywhere in the world you want on a honeymoon."

She laughed so loud she snorted, completely unlike her usual reserved self. She had Byron back and her life wasn't going to be settled, orderly, or functional, it was going to be happy. "You don't want to wait for Summer and Chance to get off their honeymoon and our parents to be there?"

"That's the definition of eloping, love, I get you all to myself."

She looked over his handsome face. "You've waited three years. Can you wait until tomorrow so we can find me a dress, you a suit that isn't ripped, and fly my parents in? Your parents are already here, and I bet we can talk Chance and Summer into stopping in for a quick wedding before they fly to Costa Rica."

He pursed his lips then smiled. "You know I'll do whatever you want, Riss. If you want, I'll wait another three years."

"I would never do that to you." She kissed him soundly and he moaned.

"Good," he said, "Because if your daddy has a shotgun, he might need to use it on me."

Marissa threw back her head and laughed. Byron took advantage of the moment to kiss her neck again. Her laughter ceased and she met his lips again. Her future husband's kissing abilities were unsurpassed. Tomorrow couldn't come soon enough.

THE FEISTY ONE BY CAMI CHECKETTS

Mr. Braxton returned with a tray of tea, coffee, and pastries. Maryn had lost herself for a few minutes in *The Last Mile* by David Baldacci. She loved that book. Now her stomach was churning too much to eat anything. Where was this guy? She'd been here for over fifteen minutes and was beginning to wonder if he planned on speaking to her at all. Typical rich jerk, thought everyone was just waiting around for him all day.

She shook out her hands and focused on snapping a few pictures of the office. If only Mr. Shaffer had allowed a camera crew to accompany her. Her paltry skills at photography would have to do.

"My apologies, ma'am. Mr. Shaffer will be joining us shortly."

"You sure about that?"

He cleared his throat. "Um, yes, ma'am. Can I offer you some tea?"

She hid a smile. This guy had missed his era and continent. He should've lived in eighteenth century England.

"No, thank you. Water would be heavenly though."

"But of course. Sparkling, bottled, or tap?"

"Is the tap good?" Being raised in Southern California, she'd hated the tap water and remembered begging her mom to put flavor in hers. Now she drank bottled.

"It is lovely, ma'am, straight out of a mountain spring."

"Oh? Tap sounds fabulous." She'd never had water from a real mountain spring, only the promises of one from The Fresh Water Man.

He left and she drummed her fingers on her jeans then stood and paced. Mr. Braxton returned with a glass of ice water. Maryn took a long drink and grinned at him. "Best water I've ever had."

"Thank you, ma'am. Can I interest you in a novel to read while you wait?"

"Be straight with me. Is he coming?"

Mr. Braxton pressed his lips together. "I assure you he is."

"Is he ditching me?"

Mr. Braxton's face reddened. "No, ma'am, he's just... freshening up."

Maryn tilted her head to the side. Tucker Shaffer cared to freshen up for her. That didn't fit his persona. "Why?"

"You arrived a bit earlier than anticipated and he was..." Mr. Braxton's mouth twisted then he spit out the word, "Sweaty."

Maryn laughed. She always tried to be a few minutes early to appointments rather than late. "I don't mind sweaty." In fact, she fully appreciated a man who was willing to sweat.

"You would've minded this," a deep voice rumbled from behind her.

Maryn whirled around to get her first look at Tucker Shaffer. My, oh, my. The man must've sweated on more than one occasion to get a build like that. Dressed in an untucked button-down shirt and jeans, he was over six feet tall with broad shoulders, a thick waist, and legs like tree trunks. She doubted anyone would dare call him overweight, but he was definitely... well-built. His dark hair was long, almost to his chin, and curled slightly. His mouth was a great shape with a bowed upper lip and full lower one and his face was that hard-working kind of handsome, the type that spent a lot of time outdoors but was still almost too good-looking. His eyes really drew her in. They were dark brown and expressive. Those eyes had stories to tell and she planned to hear them. She knew this was the interview that would guarantee her a successful career and as long as he didn't pick her up and toss her out of here, she was definitely overstaying her welcome today.

Maryn grinned at him and took a step forward with her hand outstretched. "Mr. Shaffer?"

"Tucker," his voice was almost a growl, like he didn't use it very often. He walked across the room and engulfed her smaller hand with his. Maryn wondered if she'd ever liked a handshake as much as she liked this one. He cleared his throat and his voice was clearer this time, but still deep enough that a little thrill of pleasure rushed through her. "You're Ms. Howe?"

"Maryn to you." She gave him a saucy wink.

He smiled and the effect was dynamic. No wonder he was an overnight success. She itched to take a picture, but didn't want to tick him off in the first five minutes.

Tucker released her hand and gestured to the comfortable chairs by the fire. Maryn sank into the soft leather. He sat kitty-corner to her. "Would you like something different to drink?"

Maryn shook her head. "I have this delicious water."

"Brax, a Dr. Pepper, please."

"Yes, sir."

Maryn could swear that was a sarcastic "sir". His help was interesting, to say the least.

Tucker grinned roguishly at the man. Mr. Braxton shook his head slightly and strode from the room.

Maryn focused on this enigmatic man next to her. Why was he a hermit? Everything about him screamed charisma and he was definitely handsome enough and wealthy enough to have scores of women begging for attention. She knew she'd beg if she wasn't so prideful and wasn't sort of dating James. Ah, James would have to forgive her, if Tucker Shaffer showed the slightest bit of interest, she'd be a goner. It wasn't like she'd committed to date James exclusively.

"Thank you for gracing me with your presence." That had come out kind of bratty. "I mean, I'm ecstatic to be here and be allowed to interview you. It's a pleasure."

"Wasn't really my idea." He studied his large hands as he spoke.

"Whose idea was it?"

"PR." He gave her a tilted smile that revealed a small scar in the corner of his lip. Maryn clasped her hands in her lap to resist touching that scar. Actors would replicate that sexy look and no one would blame them. Holy moly, she needed to focus.

"My PR team is a pain in the butt," he said.

A loud chortle came out before Maryn clamped her hand to her lips. "I know how that is, my editor is the same."

Mr. Braxton brought Tucker's soda.

"Thanks, Brax."

Maryn noticed the familiarity. These two were playing a part, she was sure of it.

"Sir." Mr. Braxton quickly left the room.

Tucker sipped from the can, set it on a side table, then spread his hands wide. "So, Maryn, interview away."

Maryn couldn't remember a single question she had. All she could think about was the size of those hands and secretly wish they were holding hers still. She pulled out her phone, grateful for notes and opened the app. Sadly, before she could ask any of the reasonable, well-thought out questions she'd agonized over, it popped out, "Why are you such a recluse?"

Tucker pumped his eyebrows and grinned at her. "If you had a place like this, would you want to go deal with society?"

She recognized deflection when she heard it. No matter. She'd get to the grit before the sun set and she needed to go check into The Angler's Lodge. Tomorrow she'd have to wake up early to drive the two hours to Idaho Falls and make her return flight, but she was going to enjoy today. "This is a fabulous house. Can you give me a tour?"

"Sure." Tucker stood.

Maryn rose next to him. Even with two inches on her boots, she only came to his chin. Curse being short. Tucker probably liked tall models to compliment his large stature. Not that it mattered—she was here for an exclusive interview, nothing more. She'd better remind herself of that every few minutes.

As they walked, she thought to ask one of her questions and found that she really wanted to know the answer, "What do you do to keep busy? Give me a typical day in the life of Tucker Shaffer."

"Everyone probably assumes I sit around doing nothing all day."

"If they assume that they obviously haven't seen how built you are."

He chuckled and directed her into the great room. Maryn got distracted for a minute gushing over the view and then all the different wood work. From the fireplace mantle to the wood encasing the windows to the gorgeous cabinetry, she was smitten by this house. "Let me just stand here by this beautiful fireplace for a minute and thaw out," she said. "Why's it so cold up here? It's October third for heaven's sake."

Tucker glanced down at her with a smirk. "It's snowed in September before."

Maryn shivered and moved closer to the fire and to him. "Okay, answer my question then we'll finish the tour."

Tucker rubbed his large palms together and studied the flames in the gas fireplace. "I try to balance my days—exercise, work around the house and yard, business, and programming."

She tilted her head to the side. "I've heard some tales about all the time you spend doing volunteer work. You like to fix things and teach people how to work, in addition to donating large sums of money."

"You really do your research, don't you?"

Maryn looked up and down his large frame. "You have no idea."

He blushed and she absolutely loved it. He had no clue how good-looking and powerful he was. He was so different from the wealthy men she'd met who thought they owned the world, the powerful men who thought they owned everyone in the world, and the good-looking men who thought they should own her and every other woman.

"So, for exercise, you like to..."

"Run, lift weights, box, and I get a lot of movement working outside, driving my gardeners crazy."

"Nice. I loved the gardener at the estate my mother worked on. He was so patient with me and always let me pick the flowers..." She trailed off as he listened to her like it was the most important thing he had to do today. "The programming?"

He swallowed and gave her a kind smile, not commenting on her revelation that she'd been the hired help. She was so beneath him socially it wasn't even funny. If you cared about social ladders, which she didn't.

"Everyone assumes after I designed Friend Zone I was done, but I've created a lot of other games and apps. I just market them under different names."

"Why?"

He spread his hands and smirked at her. "Avoid taxes, why else?"

She laughed. "Okay, I'll buy that. Whose names?"

"Whoever I want to share the money with—usually Mama Porter, Johnson, and Brax." He shrugged like it was no big deal.

Maryn's eyes widened. "That's pretty impressive, Tucker Shaffer. Hey. Are you just trying to impress me?"

He smiled at her. "I don't know, is it working?"

"So far it is." The warmth of the fire and the warmth of his gaze both made her a bit flushed. "Okay. I'm ready to finish the tour, then I want to sit by this fireplace and grill you some more."

Tucker blew out a long breath. "Don't you have enough information already?"

Maryn laughed. "Yeah, I'm going to print a premier article and all I've got is how you spend your days and how good-looking you are."

Tucker grinned at that and the scar in the corner of his lips was tempting her. She wanted to know how he got it, after she kissed it, that is. Whoa, she needed to focus. "Sorry," she explained. "My mouth tends to run too much."

"No, you're great. I feel very... comfortable with you."

Maryn grinned.

"But I don't like my life being on display. I'm not sure why I let them talk me into this."

"Come on, big guy, has it been that hard on you?"

He chuckled at that. "Not so far, but you know what they say about beautiful reporters?"

Maryn bit at her lip to hide a smile. "No, what's that?"

"They could talk a saint into hell."

"Oh, that's awful. I have no desire to talk anyone into that place. I'm going to heaven to be with my Granny Ellie, thank you very much." Maryn pressed her lips together. She had to stop revealing too much. Be professional, she reminded herself.

Tucker placed a hand on her back and directed her toward the front staircase again. She loved the warmth of his large palm on her back. "I'm sorry about your Granny Ellie."

"She's actually not mine, but my best friend's. Granny Ellie just adopted me and I miss her. She was the one person who always appreciated my snide comments."

Tucker looked sharply at her. "You don't have family of your own?"

"No one to brag about. I have my mom. She tried. Worked her butt off in more ways than one so I could have some sort of life." *Family of her own?* In her childish dreams.

"I'm sorry to hear that."

"No, no, no, we aren't here to talk about me." Maryn mentally shook herself. Why was she opening up to this guy? She needed her head examined. Yes, she tended to talk too much and use funny expressions, but she usually employed those techniques to put people at ease, not tell her life story. It had taken James two years to know as much about her as she'd revealed to Tucker in twenty minutes. Cripes! "Tell me more about your volunteer work. Is it always local?"

Tucker gave her an appraising look, but told her a little about his latest humanitarian trip to Ethiopia where they'd been able to dig safer wells and help some villages plant community gardens. Maryn was more and more impressed with this man. Today was looking to be one of the most interesting and productive of her career and the man at her side was looking to be a dream come true, for a reporter with good interview skills that is. Not for a woman who already had a sort of boyfriend.

Tuck had to resist touching the beautiful Maryn as they sauntered through his house. She oohed and aahed over the woodwork, the huge windows showcasing the forest and the river beyond, and the decorations that were rustic and comfortable. He'd never been around such a small person with so much energy. He liked her bold manner of speaking and he loved the way her face lit up as she talked. When he met her gaze and those blue eyes sparkled, he talked himself into believing the sparkle was just for him.

They'd finished the tour and were lounging in the enclosed, heated patio off the back of his great room. Mama Porter bustled out of the kitchen with a tray of steaming food. Tuck stood quickly and took the tray from her. "You don't need to serve us," he said.

"Of course I do. We've got a guest." She beamed at Maryn. "And she's such a beauty. Hello, love, I'm Mama Porter. It's wonderful to have you here."

Maryn stood and held out her hand. Mama Porter placed it between her plump fingers.

"Thank you. This smells exquisite. I'm Maryn."

"Oh, I know who you are. Have you got all the information you need for your article, my dear?" Mama Porter released Maryn's hand, gestured for her to sit, and started uncovering platters of orange chicken, ham-fried rice, and chow mein.

"No, actually." Maryn cocked her head to the side and pinned him with a stare. "Tucker is very skilled at evading some of the questions I need answered and getting information out of me that I don't usually share."

Tucker rubbed at his suddenly warm neck. Maryn was a professional and she'd come to get an exclusive interview. Of course she wouldn't be happy to have pictures of his house and a little bit of inside information about the different products he'd created and his latest humanitarian trip.

He'd tried all afternoon to get to know her better, but all he really obtained was she was born and raised in southern California, with her mother, but her best friend, Alyssa, and adopted Granny were her real family. She didn't surf because her best friend had a deformed foot so they'd never tried surfing, but she loved to swim in the ocean.

Mama Porter darted a gaze at him. She knew how much he appreciated his privacy, but she'd been with him for five years now and treated him like one of the sons she'd lost. "I wish I could reveal all his secrets dear, but that's not my place."

Tucker heard a low growl escape from his throat. He clamped his lips to keep it in.

Mama Porter gave him a warning look as Maryn eyed him with concern. Why didn't she jump and run away? Most women would probably be terrified of how big and unwelcoming he was. He smiled to himself. Maryn made it impossible to not be welcoming as she teased him and made him smile.

"I hope you enjoy Chinese food," Mama Porter said.

"I love it." Maryn grinned. "Thank you for dinner. I'm sure it will be delicious."

Mama Porter scurried away.

"Won't you be joining us?" Maryn asked before the patio door closed and sealed them alone again. There was a little trepidation in her voice. She *was* scared of him and who could blame her? A teeny little thing and he probably looked like an ogre with his huge body. He was evil, but she couldn't know that. No one but his closest friends knew and would ever know.

"No, dear." Mama Porter poked her head through the door. "I'll give you that chance to get him to open up."

Tucker glared at her, but she simply blew him a kiss and banged into the house. An awkward silence followed. Tucker offered Maryn the fried rice first, dishing up his plate with each dish after she'd taken what she wanted. He was pleasantly surprised that she took a decent serving size and actually started eating. The few young women he'd tried to date when he first made his money had claimed to never be hungry. He didn't understand how someone couldn't be hungry as he loved to eat almost as much as he loved to be left alone.

"So..." Maryn set down her fork and faced him bravely. "Are you going to answer any of my questions?"

"I've answered... some of them." He pushed noodles around on his plate. The fear of her discovering his secrets closed his throat and made him feel claustrophobic, like he was still hiding in a cave in Afghanistan with nothing but his pistol, semi-automatic rifle, and Johnson as protection. He took a swallow of water. "What would you like to know?"

"First of all, why are you a recluse?"

"You're some big time writer and the burning question is the same one that everyone asks me?" He bit at his cheek. He was being too harsh.

Maryn arched her delicate eyebrows and waited.

Pushing some food around on his plate, he finally muttered, "Honestly, it's just the same old story."

"Which is?"

He met her gaze and found himself falling into those blue eyes. He stuttered out the response his PR people had drilled into him, "I made my money fast and I didn't know who to trust. I surround myself with a few people who have been true to me and I stay away from the rest."

"You're right, that is a lame old story." Maryn smiled to soften her words. "Would you ever tell *me* the truth?"

Tuck blinked at her. If she kept smiling at him like that, he'd tell her a lot of things that he shouldn't. "That is the truth... okay, some of the truth."

"Did a woman break your heart?"

Tuck chuckled and forked a bite of orange chicken. "Never been close enough to a woman to allow that to happen."

"Interesting. The famous Tucker Shaffer doesn't like women?"

The orange chicken caught in his throat. He swallowed and shook his head. "I definitely *like* women." *Especially feisty blondes.* "I just haven't had an opportunity to meet the right one."

Maryn glanced outside then back at him. Her blue eyes pierced right through him and Tuck wondered what he could do to get her to stay here, with him. No. That was crazy thinking. A gorgeous, city-born woman would never be happy with his lifestyle.

"Kind of hard to find that opportunity with a guard who's a stiff, a butler who's stuck in the eighteenth century, and a cook who reminds me of Mrs. Potts from Beauty and the Beast."

"You can be Beauty and I'll be the Beast," the words were out before Tuck could stop them.

Maryn's eyes widened, but then a small smile curled her lips. "I've had worse offers."

Tuck loved the way she talked, but sometimes wasn't sure what she meant. She'd had worse offers, but had she had better? He'd checked and there was no wedding ring, but that didn't mean there was no boyfriend. Oh, he was pathetic. The first woman he truly interacted with in the past six months and he was drooling over her like a teenage boy.

"You were raised in foster care," Maryn said. "Do you keep in touch with any of your families?"

Tuck's chest tightened. They'd moved from what he would consider flirtation to his awkward childhood. Fabulous. "Only Brax."

"Mr. Braxton was one of your foster fathers?"

"Grandfather. I lived with his daughter and her family from ten to twelve years old. Brax and I had a connection and kept in touch for years. He encouraged me and believed in me when no one else did. When I had my success, it was about the same time that he was retiring from being a doctor, and his wife had passed away a few years before that, so I talked him into staying with me. He's amazing with investments and the business side of things." That was a long speech, hopefully it would satisfy her reporter curiosity.

"He's not really your butler."

"No." Tuck smiled and shook his head. "When Johnson first met him he teased that Brax was stiff and proper like an English butler. They have a bet going when we have guests. Guess Brax won this time."

"There's a story behind all of your staff, isn't there?"

"All three of them?"

"Three?" Her eyes widened and she glanced around. "Only three? How do you maintain all the property you have with a staff of three?"

He shrugged. "I pay caretakers when I'm not at one of my homes. When we're living there we have a maid service come in twice a week and keep a gardener on staff, but all of us pitch in to upkeep the house and yard of wherever we live."

"So the stiff outside isn't really a guard dog?"

Tuck laughed so hard his side hurt. He never laughed like that. "Maybe Johnson won the bet with Brax after all. He's a buddy from college. He enrolled in the Army to put himself through school, was deployed to Afghanistan for eighteen months." He clenched his fist, not sure why he was revealing all of this. He cleared his throat and looked down, lest she see the truth in his eyes. "He saw and was commanded to do some things that scarred him pretty good. He likes to patrol the property and watch the cameras, but only uses his weapons now to hunt and pretend to be a guard when people stop by. He's brilliant with real estate and takes care of all of those kinds of transactions for us. He's also more social than the rest of us and gets out and makes friends wherever we live." No reason to tell her the things he and Johnson had seen together.

"Does sweet Mama Porter cook *and* clean?"

"I do a lot of the day to day stuff and everyone pitches in, then like I said I have a cleaning service come in twice a week and scour the place."

Maryn took a slow breath. "You're not what I expected, Tucker Shaffer."

"Is anyone ever what you expect?" Tuck wondered if she liked what she learned about him or liked her original perception of him more.

"Good point. So, tell me more."

He laughed and shook his head. No way was she getting much more out of him than she'd already gotten. Unless she was willing to go on a date with him sometime soon. "I've already told you more than any reporter I've ever met."

"That wasn't tough, you've never talked to any reporters."

"Good thing I liked you the first time I saw you or I would've thrown you out."

"Would you really?"

Tuck had to look down. He folded his napkin and placed it on his near-empty plate. "Probably."

"Why do you want people to be afraid of you?"

Tuck hunched over, feeling like she'd punched him in the gut. "It's just easier that way."

"So the mysterious, ultra-wealthy loner who frightens everyone away is really a softy who cleans toilets and only allows those he's trusted for years close to him." She leaned toward him and he smelled a fresh, clean scent. It reminded him of sunshine and lilacs.

Tuck lifted his hands. "I don't clean toilets."

She smiled. "Why keep the world at arm's length?"

THE FEISTY ONE BY CAMI CHECKETTS

"How much of this are you going to print? You aren't writing anything down."

She tapped her head. "Near perfect memory. At least when I care about what I'm learning. I promise I'll send you the article before it goes to print for your approval."

"I really don't want all my secrets out to the world." His voice dropped and he should've been embarrassed as he said, "If you were asking for Maryn Howe instead of for *The Rising Star*, I might be persuaded to reveal a secret or two."

She tilted her head to the side. That silky blonde hair trailed over her shoulder and Tuck wanted more than anything to entwine his fingers in it.

"Are we that friendly?" she asked.

Tuck suddenly realized what a fool he was, coming onto the reporter who only wanted any dirt he was willing to reveal. He needed to get a social life. Maybe he could find a nice girl at the local church they attended on Sundays or let Johnson set him up. Tuck hadn't dated much the past few years, but obviously it was time if he could feel an immediate connection and attraction to someone who needed to be kept farther than arm's length.

"Why didn't you show me the third floor?" Maryn asked.

Tuck drew in a slow breath. "That's my private suite. I don't show it to anyone, most of all to reporters."

"What if I was asking as Maryn Howe not as *The Rising Star*? I promise not to take any pictures or print anything you tell me on that floor."

Tuck knew he was a lonely, depraved idiot, but it wasn't like she was going to open drawers, look through his desk, or find everything he wanted to hide. He stood, offered her his hand, and said, "Okay."

Maryn tried not to stare at Tucker as they ascended the grand staircase then kept winding up and up. Glancing out the windows, she could see snow swirling in the air. She sucked in a breath. "Look at that! It's so pretty. I've never seen snow before."

"Really?"

"California girl."

He grinned at her. Maryn smiled back, but then suddenly realized she'd have to drive in this snow. How terrifying, but she couldn't leave now, she was just getting to the good stuff with Tucker. No way was a little white fluff going to interrupt that. She'd just have to be extra careful and pray the snow stopped.

Tucker rested his hand on her back, but when she glanced up, he quickly dropped it. He was... prickly and handsome and he just had presence. Definitely more interesting than any man she'd ever encountered. His eyes were so full of secrets she felt like she was wading through half-truths every time he told her something. What was he hiding? He'd been in the Army with Johnson; she knew that from her research. Why lie and say that only Johnson had scars from service? What had he done in Afghanistan that had affected him so deeply? If only she could snoop a little more. Instant guilt arose. Tucker had been very kind and accommodating to her. He didn't deserve his dirt displayed for the world to mock. Whatever she discovered by the time she left here today, she vowed to paint him in a good light.

Tucker opened the double doors and Maryn's jaw dropped open. They entered a sitting area first with floor to ceiling windows. Fat snowflakes floated from the sky. She should say her goodbyes and find her hotel before the roads got too dangerous, but she couldn't force herself to leave yet. There was still much more to learn about Tucker and she wanted to be the one to learn it. Oddly enough, the article was no longer the number one reason for spending more time with him.

The walls of the room were knotty pine and all the furnishings were a deep reddish-brown leather, except for a mahogany desk and a cherry wood mantle over the granite-surround of the fireplace. There was an archway to her right into a bedroom with a massive bed and she could see an arched bathroom entrance and a walk-in closet beyond that.

"This is amazing," Maryn breathed.

Tucker's face relaxed into a smile. "Thank you. My private sanctuary."

"Thank you for sharing it with me. I won't... take any pictures or write about it." Their eyes met and held and she whispered, "I promise." Many wealthy people had private rooms they didn't want on display, but there was something more here, she felt it. She would keep her promise, even from James and Alyssa. Thinking of James made her feel guilty. He wouldn't appreciate the way she was so intrigued by this man. She needed to keep this attraction under control, but when Tucker nodded his thanks and gave her a brief smile, darn if that scar next to his lip didn't appear. Thoughts of James were pushed far away.

Tucker gestured toward the overstuffed leather seats by the gas fireplace. A quick click of a button on the remote and the fire sprang to life. Maryn sank down and studied the churning snowstorm outside. It was truly beautiful. "This is perfect. If only I didn't have to drive in the snow and could sit here with a cup of cocoa and a Baldacci novel."

"I think you're going to get your wish. These snowstorms can be vicious. You'll have to stay until it passes."

The muscles in Maryn's neck tightened. She'd wanted that invite and she definitely didn't want to drive in the snow, but what if things became awkward? "Oh, I couldn't possibly... stay."

She felt his gaze on her and almost gasped at the amused and honestly wicked glint in his brown eyes.

"I've had enough bad press." Tucker spread his hands, the picture of innocence, except for the searing look in those eyes. "I'm not going to add, 'threw a reporter out of his house in a blizzard where she slid off the road and received gaping wounds then caught hypothermia and died,' to the stack."

Maryn took a long breath. Her gaze returned to the lodge pole pines being loaded with snow. Whereas the view used to include the river, it was now impossible to see past the first row of trees. She'd never experienced snow, but would assume this was what the newscasters meant when they said a whiteout. The storm had come on quick.

"I don't want to impose," she murmured.

"Mama Porter would be thrilled," he said.

"What about you?" she asked before she could stop herself, curse her errant tongue.

"I would be... grateful for the opportunity."

"Opportunity to do what?"

"Get to know my beautiful reporter better."

"And here everyone claims you have no social skills."

Tucker's eyes darkened but his smile remained in place. "If you stay, you'll be able to tell them a different story."

Goosebumps rose on Maryn's arms. She wasn't sure what story she was going to tell when this adventure was over, but the idea of spending more time with him had every nerve singing. She licked her lips and then forced herself to focus on the beautiful scenery outside, lest he notice her drooling over him.

Tucker's phone rang. "Excuse me," he said, standing and walking into his bedroom.

Maryn also stood and walked around, looking at the artwork he'd chosen to display. She was shocked to see one of her friend, Alyssa's, photographs on the wall. This man liked Baldacci novels and A.A.'s photography. Of course, Alyssa was now married to Beckham Taylor, but she still did her artwork under A.A. Maryn was beginning to think that Tucker was too good to be true. Why had everyone made him out to be a social cipher and a jerk?

Tucker was still talking in the other room, something about a grizzly bear on the property which had entered through the river. It sounded like the guard dog, Johnson, was monitoring the situation. She shivered. She'd never seen a bear except for at the zoo, but they still gave her nightmares. Taking Tucker up on his offer to stay inside this safe, beautiful house sounded better and better.

She paused at an antique roll top desk nestled against one wall. She wanted to open it in the worst way. Curse reporter instincts. She'd promised Tucker she wouldn't reveal anything she learned in his rooms, so what would it hurt to look?

Unable to resist, she made sure Tucker wasn't looking, and slowly lifted the cover. Photos were scattered over the desk, all of them snap-shots of beautiful children near a cave entrance. The scenery was brown, possibly desert. They appeared to be of Arab descent. Maryn wondered what the connection was to Tucker. She picked up a picture of a darling boy, who couldn't have been more than eight or nine.

Turning the print over, she read, "Murdered by Lieutenant Tucker Shaffer."

She gasped and dropped the picture like it was a hot ember from the fire. Her heart thumped louder and louder. Had she really seen that? It couldn't be true. Tucker seemed like such a nice guy.

Leaning back, she spied Tucker inclining against the four-poster bed with the phone to his ear. Maryn picked up a snapshot of a teenage girl with flowing black hair and a beautiful smile. She slowly turned it over and the same words were written in bold marker, "Murdered by Lieutenant Tucker Shaffer." Her eyes darted over the pictures, ice rubbing along her spine. There were at least half a dozen of the pictures. He couldn't possibly have... killed all these children?

Cold fear pricked at her neck. She needed to get out of this house. "Okay, girl," she muttered to herself, "play it cool and then make a quick exit. He'll never know."

Setting the picture down, she grabbed the top and started rolling it down. It squeaked. She gasped and moved it slower, saying a quick prayer for help. She noticed the silence a split second before she could feel his breath on her cheek.

"Did you find what you were looking for?" he asked, his voice a low growl.

Maryn released the desktop, whipped around to face him, and tried to back up, but she was pressed into the desk. "I'm sorry. I didn't mean to see. I was just looking around. They were sitting right on your desk." She hated that her voice squeaked but her throat was closing off.

He leaned into her space, his dark eyes snapping. "Did you find what you were looking for?" he repeated.

"I-I think I need to go."

"Screw the bad publicity," he snarled. "You think I'm going to let you leave now? Tell the whole world about what a monster Tucker Shaffer really is?" His lips curled into a feral grin. His brown eyes had turned black and cold.

Maryn's breath was coming in short bursts. He wasn't touching her, but she felt like she was standing in the shadow of a calculating animal and he was going to lash out at any second. Being mugged last summer was less terrifying than the look in Tucker Shaffer's eyes. How had the warm, friendly man morphed into this beast?

Without thinking, she stomped on his foot with the heel of her red boots. He cried out, probably more in surprise than pain. She ducked under his arm and sprinted out the door. She ran down the three flights of steps without looking back to see if he pursued. Mr. Braxton was in the office and glanced up in surprise when she yanked the front door open.

"Ms. Howe?" He hurried into the foyer. "Where are you going? There's a bear and—"

"I'll take my chances," she muttered, flying down the front steps and ignoring whatever else Mr. Braxton was trying to say. Her little red rental car was still sitting there in the circle. At least they hadn't moved her car and kept her prisoner. There was something very wrong with this house and the people inside.

Maryn slipped on the snow and went down hard. Her elbow and knee slammed onto the wet pavement. She hauled herself up, limping and sliding the remaining steps to her car, these cute boots were not made for snow. She peered through the thick snow, waiting for a grizzly bear to rip her apart. Not sure if she was more scared of a real grizzly bear out in this forest, or the beast of a man inside the house. She chanced a glance up, up to the third story. Tucker Shaffer stood at the window.

Read more or buy *The Feisty One* here.

THE ADVENTUROUS ONE BY JEANETTE LEWIS

"What's ahead for you?" Taylor asked as they sat on the restaurant patio with sandwiches and salads. They were at a small round table and had pulled their chairs so close they were almost touching. The sun was warm on their faces and a small breeze ruffled their hair. Taylor thought of the skydiving and wanted to go back.

Lane picked at his pasta salad with his fork. "I don't know. Same old, same old I guess. Work. What about you?"

Her face fell. "I'm not sure. I mean, I submit my travel plans to my editor a year in advance, so I guess I'll be picking up where I left off in my schedule when I leave here. I just ..." She trailed off, unsure how to phrase it.

"You're wondering what's ahead for us?" he asked softly.

Heart in her throat, she nodded. The differences between this day with Lane and the day on the boat with Brent were stark in her mind. No guilt, no harsh words, no second guessing, no nerves—except for the good kind. Just being with him, just looking at him, sent thrills shooting through her core and goosebumps parading up her arms. It was embarrassing, really, though if he'd noticed, he hadn't commented.

Lane put his fork down and reached for her hand. His fingers closed around hers, warm and strong. "I don't know," he admitted. "I really like you. No, scratch that, I more than like you."

Taylor gave up all pretense of playing it cool. "I more than like you too," she whispered.

He flashed her a smile, then he was leaning toward her and she was leaning toward him. There was a moment, right before she closed her eyes, when she could see the flecks of gold in his hazel eyes, the fringe of lashes around them. He smelled clean and soapy and faintly like pine trees. Then her eyes fluttered closed and his lips brushed hers, warm and soft.

She didn't remember dropping her fork, but suddenly her hands were free, sliding up the warm contours of his arms, over his muscular shoulders, and into the thick hair at the back of his head. Heat and longing exploded through her body as she wound her fingers into his hair as his mouth claimed hers. He tasted like cola and salad dressing, like spending a lazy summer day in a hammock, like swimming in a warm hot springs, like freedom and passion and love.

Lane's arms were around her, one clamped at her waist, the other at the back of neck, guiding her head so their mouths moved in sync.

"Get a room!" Someone hollered, another diner on the patio, and they broke apart. For a moment they stared at each other, unsure whether to be embarrassed by so much PDA, but then Taylor giggled. She didn't care.

Lane laughed. "Sorry about that," he called to the person who yelled. "Can you blame me though?"

The man chuckled, shaking his head, and went back to his lunch.

"Wow," Lane leaned forward, resting his forehead against Taylor's. "Can we do that again?"

She couldn't quite catch her breath. "Come with me," she whispered, before she could think.

His eyes grew big. "What do you mean?"

It was pure impulse, brought on by desire and raging hormones, but more than that, the knowledge that *this* was what she'd wanted from the moment she'd seen him again. She wanted to explore the world with this man at her side. "No expectations," she added quickly, seeing the confusion in his eyes. "We'd get separate rooms, like when

Summer and I travel with her boyfriends. I just ... I think it would be really fun to have you along, and I think you'd like it. It could be the way it was, at the outdoor club, the two of us, together. I want you to come, *need* you to come ... need you," she finished shakily.

He ran one hand down the curve of her cheek and sat back. "What's your next trip?" He asked.

"I cut my trip to Mexico short to come help with Grandma, so I have a couple more weeks free, but then in August, I start the Appalachian Trail." The thought of having Lane along turned it from an exciting hike into a magical adventure.

"The Appalachian Trail is over two thousand miles long," Lane said. "You're hiking *all* of it?"

"Not the whole thing," she said. "I haven't finalized my route yet, but I'm planning to be in New England by autumn to see the leaves. Depending on how much longer Grandma needs me, I might start there and work my way south. What do you think?"

She'd thought it would be exactly like the kind of thing Lane would love. But his face fell and he stared past her at their reflection in the restaurant windows. "Yeah, sounds great," he said slowly. "If I could walk more than a mile without needing to rest. Or if I could even get up an incline as steep as a dopey bridge in a city park."

"So that's where my friend comes in," Taylor urged. "She can help you get the equipment you need so you *can* do that kind of stuff, don't you see?" Her palms were clammy—please let him say yes. Please let him see this was possible.

But Lane shook his head and poked at his salad again with his fork. "I can't," he muttered. "I can't take charity."

Taylor groaned in frustration. "Will you shelve your silly pride for a few minutes," she urged.

It was the wrong thing to say. Lane's head shot up and his eyes turned cold. "My *pride* is what got me through," he said quietly. "It's about the only thing I have left."

"But it doesn't have to be that way," she said, on a roll now that she couldn't stop, didn't want to stop. "You don't have to just accept this is the way your life is now, there are still lots of things you could be doing, lots of adventures you could be having, if you'll let yourself."

"I'll get there, Taylor," he said firmly. "But on my own terms."

She shook her head, tears brimming in her eyes. "No you won't. You'll go on working in your stupid little office and struggling along and never doing anything you've dreamed about because you're too stubborn to realize someone tried to give you exactly what you needed and you refused."

His hand clenched around his fork. "You have no idea what it's like," he grated.

"You're right, I don't. What you've been through is beyond imagining and I have no frame of reference for it. But I do know what it's like to be hurt ... so devastated that you think you're beyond repair. I've been there, and it took a long time, but I learned you can't let one terrible thing define you for the rest of your life."

"It's not the same," he insisted. "You didn't lose a third of your body."

"That's true," Taylor said carefully, sensing dangerous territory. "Something horrendous happened to you, more awful than I can even imagine. But you're more than your legs, you're more than one day, one decision, one tragic accident. You have all kinds of things about you that have nothing to do with any of that, but you're ignoring all the good things to focus only on this one bad thing." She put her hand on his arm, trying to soften the words. "You can pay her back if that's what you're worried about, but don't waste these best years of your life. Once they're gone, they're gone. Money is a renewable commodity, but time isn't."

His Adam's apple bobbed as he swallowed hard, looking as if he was on the verge of tears, just as she was.

"Please?" she whispered.

He shook his head. "I can't."

Read more or buy *The Adventurous One* here.

ABOUT THE AUTHOR

Cami is a part-time author, part-time exercise consultant, part-time housekeeper, full-time wife, and overtime mother of four adorable boys. Sleep and relaxation are fond memories. She's never been happier.

Sign up for Cami's newsletter to receive a free ebook copy of *The Feisty One: A Billionaire Bride Pact Romance* and information about new releases, discounts, and promotions here.

www.camichecketts.com
cami@camichecketts.com

ALSO BY CAMI CHECKETTS

Rescued by Love: Park City Firefighter Romance

Reluctant Rescue: Park City Firefighter Romance

The Resilient One: Billionaire Bride Pact Romance

The Feisty One: Billionaire Bride Pact Romance

The Independent One: Billionaire Bride Pact Romance

The Protective One: Billionaire Bride Pact Romance

The Faithful One: Billionaire Bride Pact Romance

The Daring One: Billionaire Bride Pact Romance

Pass Interference: A Last Play Romance

How to Love a Dog's Best Friend

Oh, Come On, Be Faithful

Shadows in the Curtain: Billionaire Beach Romance

Caribbean Rescue: Billionaire Beach Romance

Cozumel Escape: Billionaire Beach Romance

Cancun Getaway: Billionaire Beach Romance

Onboard for Love: Billionaire Beach Romance

Protect This

Blog This

Redeem This

The Broken Path

Dead Running

Dying to Run

Running Home

Full Court Devotion: Christmas in Snow Valley

A Touch of Love: Summer in Snow Valley

Made in the USA
Columbia, SC
16 July 2023

20539659R00095